A Harlequin Romance

BLAZE OF SILK

by

MARGARET WAY

HARLEQUIN BOOKS

Toronto • Canada New York • New York

BLAZE OF SILK

First published in 1970 by Mills & Boon Limited,
17 - 19 Foley Street, London, England

Harlequin Canadian edition published June, 1971
Harlequin U.S. edition published September, 1971

All the characters in this book have no existence outside the imagination of the Author, and have no relation whatsoever to anyone bearing the same name or names. They are not even distantly inspired by any individual known or unknown to the Author, and all the incidents are pure invention.

Standard Book Number: 373-51500-6.

Printed in Canada

CHAPTER ONE

DANA'S father led the way through the thinning crowd, his hand closed tightly on her elbow. There was pride, even arrogance in the set of his head and the jut of his chin, which was moulded along perfect classical lines—an incongruous note in an otherwise rugged dark face. The same pride was reflected in the tilt of his daughter's blonde head and the ominous sparkle to her long, amber eyes, clear and beautiful beneath their dark, arching brows. Dana's chin and its angle were her father's, and the only visible aspect of their relationship.

Even as they approached the ballroom a small group broke up and dispersed, their faces a mixture of dismay and wariness. Dana glanced sharply at her father, her breath catching on a protest. Sloan Gregory's strong, high-cheekboned face was taut with anger barely under control. These were his *friends* who were now cold-shouldering him—the racing fraternity, the devoted followers of the Turf, owners, breeders, trainers, jockeys, pressmen, together with their womenfolk. The same *friends* who twelve months ago had given him a standing ovation for his third consecutive Cup win. It had been a treasured memory! But what a reversal fate had in store for him. Tonight he was a man under suspicion, facing a full inquiry into the running of Prince Akura, the national idol and unplaced favourite for Australia's supreme social and sporting event, the Melbourne Cup.

Beside him, Dana felt her father's humiliation with stunning impact. She drew a deep, steadying breath, using every scrap of her will power to keep herself from shaking. But why show the sick panic that climbed in her? she decided. Just keep yourself moving, girl, she told herself. One foot after the other. A sense of strangeness hovered around her almost as though she were watching a play in which she was also one of the players.

How many times in the past had she anticipated this evening, this *victory* evening, which was to have been her social debut, but never in a thousand daydream versions had she imagined it would be fraught with such bitter tension, the savage need to hold up one's head and keep it there. Hadn't her father always said: 'There's nothing lower than a fallen idol.' How right he had been! Once you had a champion in your stable you and your horse became public property. Now the public had rejected him.

The room spun around her in a dazzling kaleidoscope of wealth and beauty, high flight fashion. Faces receded into shadow, blurred and anonymous, but the eyes were everywhere, avid, speculative, coldly denouncing. Dana swallowed dryly as the events of the afternoon flashed before her eyes with intense clarity—the tumult and confusion at the champion's poor performance, the unanimous conclusion of foul play that had swept through the crowd like an electrical impulse.

Prince Akura, the powerful chestnut with four white legs and a big white blaze, the three-to-one favourite with a string of classic wins behind him, had faltered badly at the outset, losing the race while carrying on his back the fortunes of a nation. But Dana knew her father so well that she never had the most fleeting element of doubt about him. Her father was a man of integrity, a man above suspicion even with the evidence piled against him. Sloan Gregory loved his horses, lived for them, never tired of telling of the thrill and pleasure of preparing a thoroughbred for the great classics, then watching him race and demonstrate his great heart and stamina. Prince Akura, the pride of the famous Rankine Stud, had been such a horse!

Abruptly Sloan Gregory came to a halt, shaking his head as though to clear it. Then, despite his avowed intention to see the night out, swung back the way he had come. Dana quickened her pace, feeling as sick and shaken as if she had just run a mile. She moved swiftly beside her father, her beautiful gown, her first formal gown, swirling round her feet in a mist of topaz. The tears beat helplessly behind her eyes. They should never have come to the ball, she knew, but she had been powerless to prevent it. Her father went his own way in all things, as perhaps a man should. Embarrassment and tension followed their path. Once or twice Dana thought she heard their name being called, felt a would-be sympathetic hand touch her arm in an attempt to impede their flight, but her father was blind and indifferent now to everything save his desire to quit the scene of his former triumphs.

In the beautiful square entrance hall their progress was impeded by the arrival of two late-coming guests. Dana became aware of two figures, both in their fashion very striking men. Her dismayed eyes fell away from the familiar rough-hewn features and shaggy silver mane of Tod Rankine, owner of Prince Akura and the Rankine Stud. Her nails dragged into the soft flesh of her palms. Almost feverishly her eyes met those of his companion, finding the stranger's own gaze upon her as though inadvertently she had caught and held his attention. She looked back at him unable to move or think. He was tall, very dark, very elegant, with lean incisive features. It was a sombre face, but somehow exciting, with an arrogance beyond bearing in the way his brilliant dark eyes ran over her before slowly turning away to look at her father with cold deliberation.

There was a kind of contempt in that probing scrutiny, in the sharply etched line of his mouth, beautiful and quite ruthless. Dana bristled, her vision blurring. A flame of hostility swept over her in great waves, instilling a fierce desire to lash out and hurt someone as she and her father had been hurt. The intensity of her feelings flashed out of her eyes. Colour burned over her high cheekbones. For the moment, her burning sense of injustice seemed to invigorate her, giving her the assurance she so badly needed.

'Would you mind standing out of my way,' she began coldly, then, meeting the stranger's eyes, knew herself defeated. There was a dangerous flicker in that dark, sombre gaze, a kind of knowledge of her and her innermost feelings.

Antagonism, instant and magnetic, flared beween them. Their eyes held for an interminable minute before Dana looked away, breathless, with the illogical feeling that the world had tilted for her and would never come right again.

Vaguely she heard her father's voice, remote and dreamlike, felt the increased pressure on her forearm. They moved out into the dark night with its powdering of stars, leaving Tod Rankine to stare after them speechlessly, the anger settling down in his face. He shuddered, the soft night air cooling his outraged feelings. Not until this very day would he have thought it possible for Sloan Gregory to be caught up in even the merest whisper of doubt—not a man with Sloan's great love of horses, his air of intense dedication. Well, every man had his price!

Tod Rankine's hand clenched and unclenched at his side, his heart pumping heavily. He was badly shaken, but there was no point in upsetting himself further. Still, it was a pity he had to cut young Dana. The little he had seen of her he liked. She was clever and spirited with all the promise of true beauty. She would make a fine woman if she could get clear of her father's influence.

His mind churned endlessly over the shock of the day's events. How could this have happened to Prince Akura, the pride of his stud, his wonderful stayer? How could Sloan have conspired to pull down a champion? A shudder passed through his heavy frame; a cry of muffled regret and anger for the irretrievably lost. He felt Brett take hold of his elbow, steering him towards the glittering rose and gold of the foyer. His nephew's voice was low and soothing, almost hypnotic in its persuasiveness.

'Take it easy now, Tod. You can safely leave your friend to the stewards.' The cool, decisive voice hardened. 'A pity about your little blonde. She's taking it hard, like she'll take most things in life.' His tone sharpened with humour as he glanced down at the older man. 'High-strung, mettlesome, in need of schooling?'

Tod Rankine threw off his slightly haunted preoccupation with an effort. It did not good to brood. Heaven knew, he had been in the upsets of the racing game long enough. For the first time that evening a smile escaped him. 'Not a word about young Dana, my boy. She's a thoroughbred, full of charm and animation. An admirable young creature.' He shook his heavy silver head. 'But her father! My God! a pity, a great pity!' Resolutely he fought for a degree of composure, a staccato pulse beating in his temple. The two men passed into the ballroom where they were immediately swept up by a high-flying set. A semblance of gaiety returned to the ballroom.

A few hundred yards away Sloan Gregory started the engine with a roar and the car swung out under a low archway into the broad street. There were cars parked on either side of it and a beautiful old cathedral flung itself upwards in sweeping flying buttresses, its soaring steeple standing delicately against the soft purple night.

Dana settled more firmly in her seat, her eyes fixed on the red rear light of the car in front of them. It was so strange to be hiding from other people's eyes. Strange and unnatural. The dim glow from the dashboard showed her father's face tight and weary. They clung together in a thought-crowded silence, depression settling over them like a tangible thing.

Part of Sloan Gregory concentrated on his driving. The rest buzzed and twisted and shouted with conjecture, doubt, helpless anger, all battling together inside his aching head. Tomorrow was the inquiry and after that—what?

CHAPTER TWO

'For God's sake keep up on the track, Paddy.' Dana straightened up and clutched the side of the old utility.

'Just dodging the rough stuff, love.' Paddy Bank, her father's trusted, permanent help, continued to rattle recklessly on and off the bush track leading to the property.

Dana let out a yelp, a mixture of laughter and alarm. The utility flashed in and out of the red-blossoming bottle-brush where Dana could have sworn no car would fit, and back up on to the track again. As often as she rode with Paddy she still found his 'going bush' quite nerve-racking. The old vehicle gathered itself for its crawl up the hill and the mad hurtle down the other side, while Paddy played hit and run with the road, his hands clenched on the wheel.

They clattered over a cattle grid that set Dana's teeth rattling, and shot off a narrow side track where a big goanna four feet long scuttled for its life in among the big shady paperbarks. A proud, untamed sun struck through the tops of the trees where birds flapped, and fed and fought, with only a stab of scarlet or a burst of blue and gold to make their presence.

Paddy took his eye off the road to glance at his companion. 'Beautiful, isn't it, love?' Dana gave a startled yelp as an ironbark loomed up in front of them. 'Easy, love,' Paddy spoke soothingly to her, then swinging the utility was once more on the road. Over towards the rich creek flats the cattle stood brisket-high in the long green grass, their placid white faces turned towards the commotion, and up among the glossy green leaves of the kurrajong a pair of jackasses burst into raucous laughter.

'Just listen to them! Yes, it's beautiful all right, love,' Paddy answered himself, his eyes on the distant blue and purple of the ranges that marked Mareeba's western boundary. Dana relaxed and smiled, her mouth tilting delightfully. Paddy was a cattleman without peer in the district, a very tall spare man with humorous blue eyes set in a maze of wrinkles, but his method of driving was unusual to say the least. Even so he had never been known to even graze a wallaby in twenty years on and off the road. Dana kept both feet firmly planted on the floor as they started the run into the homestead.

The blue lagoon was thrusting with waterlilies, magnificent blooms cupping the clear sheet of water a half a mile long and nearly as wide, and rocking to the consecutive dives of a flock of corellas that loaded the branches of the blue-gums.

Paddy accelerated madly for the run up to the homestead, craning forward in concentration. Mareeba was set on a gentle rise overlooking the creek and surrounded by a summer profusion of gardens and great shade trees of gum, acacia, peperinas and kurrajongs—magnificent shade trees that had been standing long before Dana had been born, long before gardens had been set at their feet.

Sloan Gregory was sitting on the wide verandah sorting out the morning's mail. He lifted his head at their noisy approach and came down the stairs, the broad smile on his face that Paddy Bank's antics never failed to put there.

'All in one piece, I see,' he sketched a salute and opened the door for Dana, bending to kiss the silken curve of her cheek. 'What's doing today, Paddy?' he looked at his head man.

Paddy squinted his eyes in the radiance of daylight. 'I thought I'd bring in the scrubbers. Every cow in its proper place is my motto.' The car bucked under his hands. 'All right with you, boss?'

'You just get after them,' Sloan smiled, and stood back from the car, hastily pulling Dana with him, as Paddy put the utility into reverse with feverish intensity. They both smiled and waved as their head man took off with a burst of bravado.

'I don't know how he does it,' Sloan laughed, and put his arm around Dana's shoulders, leading her back up to the shade of the verandah. Bougainvilleas cascaded in a brilliant red torrent over one end of it, fell over a trellis and clustered over the framework of the silver glittering windmill that pumped water from the creek to the twin storage tanks at the side of the house.

'Anything special happen?' Dana smoothed back her long blonde hair and sat down in the chair beside her father.

'Another one of these.' Sloan hit the side of his knee with the envelope, pausing significantly. They both knew what 'one of these' meant: overtures to return to the turf, to take up where he had left off three years ago in happier circumstances as the country's top trainer. Dana looked away to the creek, her mind going over the time they had spent at Mareeba, the Queensland cattle station her father had bought on the spot from old Colonel Faxon, a one-time notable breeder of racehorses.

'You love it, don't you?' Sloan said rather absently. He was gazing out at the lagoon also without really seeing it.

Dana's glance sharpened and met her father's.

'Of course I do, Dad. It's been a haven to us.'

She offered no further comment, allowing him to come to the heart of the matter in his own time. A white cockatoo, sulphur-crested, spun out and hung motionless quite near in the curve of a kurrajong. The silence lengthened until on an impulse Dana got up and wound her arms around her father's neck.

'But even a haven can pall, is that it, Dad? *You* miss the old life, don't you?—the special magic when the horses come into the birdcage, down along the track to the stalls in front of the lawn. Chestnuts, bays, glistening like newly minted coins, necks arched, high stepping, the glimmer of silk, satin jackets, all the race day finery, crowding the fence.'

She rubbed her head fondly against her father's cheek while he patted her arm, overly conscious of the colour pictures Dana was evoking. Dana sighed, knowing his thoughts, then uncurled herself, moving back to the wrought-iron railing.

'We can always go back, Dad. No charge was ever laid against the Prince's connections. One inexplicable failure can't be allowed to weigh against you indefinitely. I'm not the only one to share that opinion, it seems. You're wanted where you really belong.'

Sloan Gregory shrugged his shoulders negligently though he was feeling anything but relaxed. These letters were unsettling just as he had got used to this new life ... or almost. Mareeba was a fine property. If he wasn't exactly a born cattleman his herd would find favour with any lover of good Herefords. The cattle were in top condition, sleek-coated and docile, and his horses were the best this side of the black stump. But it wasn't the same. Dana knew how it was with him, none better. It had proved impossible for him to stifle his great love of the turf, the world of the thoroughbred, the blazing speed and spectacular beauty of his beloved horses.

Nostalgia swept over him and a brightly illumined picture of his last champion, Prince Akura, the now magnificent stud stallion he had bought as a yearling for Tod Rankine. But Tod was gone. To his bitter regret they had never even exchanged a voluntary word at the inquiry, and now the famous Rankine nurseries had changed hands. He himself had long since given up trying to fathom the reason for the big stallion's failure. Such conjecture as had once clung to him, despite any found evidence, had now evaporated. He was still needed, his record had not been bettered, neither his method. An owner could spend a fortune on a horse, engage the best jockey, but it was the trainer who brought the horse to the peak of perfection.

Dana watched her father's expressive face with increasing attention. He was so proud, temperamental, headstrong to a fault. Three years ago nothing less than two thousand miles away had been enough for him. One of the few to believe in his complete noncomplicity had been old Colonel Faxon, a man who prided himself on being an expert judge of men and horses. It was the Colonel who had offered Mareeba with its running fire of hooves and stockwhips, once Sloan Gregory had bitterly and publicly announced his intention to retire from the turf.

Within a month of the inquiry, a nine days' wonder,

they had come up to Queensland, leaving their hardest days behind them.

Dana ran a contemplative finger down her short straight nose, observing her father's air of intense preoccupation. He was in the peak of physical condition but he looked fine-drawn, the deep lines running from nose to mouth more pronounced than usual.

'There's no reason why we have to stay, Dad.'

'But you love it, dear. You'd miss it.'

'Not a bit,' Dana lied cheerfully, and raised her eyes to a flight of wild duck sailing across the sun. Would she miss it? The great Outback, the smell and the heat of it; the peace and the freedom; the thrill when the rains came drenching the trees, flashing with superb lorikeets and rosellas. The waterholes flecked with pink and blue-petalled waterlilies, the wonderful sunsets that assaulted the eye. Oh, yes, she would miss it.

'Not a bit,' she repeated, and smiled at her father, her eyes a warm loving amber. Her father smiled too on a fresh wave of love for her. What a joy and a comfort she had been to him these past eight years since Abby died in his arms leaving him broken and bereft. But Abby would have wanted something different for her little girl. It was a good life out here, but too far from the bright urban life, the fun and the parties, the social establishment that most young girls seemed to crave for. Yet Dana seemed happy enough and she did love the bush. He made a curious heartwarming gesture towards her and said gently:

'You're a good girl, Dana. I could never have managed without you.'

Dana nodded, her eyes crinkling with mischief.

'I know, Dad, but that doesn't solve anything.'

Sloan sat bolt upright with a flash of his old self.

'Well, you tell me, darling, you so often do.'

'It's up to me, isn't it?' Dan said impetuously with her uncanny knack of being one jump ahead. 'You want me to make the decision for you. You're a bit above yourself, Dad, like some of your own horses.'

Her father gave a short laugh.

'Perhaps I am. But it's not so strange that I want something better for you. You're a beautiful girl, Dana, it's my duty to provide the right opportunities for you. You need young companionship, surely?'

'You're getting off the track, Dad, as well you know.'

Sloan Gregory shot his daughter a glance, then stared at the floor.

'All right then, it's quite simple really. I made my decision three years ago, announced it publicly and said my piece while I was at it. If and when we go back to the city it will be for a far different reason than mixing myself up in the racing game again. Out here, at least I know who my friends are, they see clearer and further.'

Dana's amber eyes were upon him with that searching quizzical look she so often gave him, so he sidestepped any further soul-searching by asking after her trip into the town.

Dana sat back in her chair, seemingly content to bring her father back to the present. They sat and discussed the gossip of the district before Dana went inside to prepare lunch. Alone, her father went over the contents of his latest letter again. It was all so very unsettling that he should be approached like this, just as he had put aside all thoughts of making a comeback.

Under the peperinas it was deliciously cool, spiked with the aromatic scent of the bush. Dana rode along the well-defined tracks that cut through the bush to the principal watering places with a wonderful sense of well being. She was an expert horsewoman and these morning rides were a great joy to her. It was fine country around Mareeba, good grazing country where her ebony mare, Sweet Pepper, swished knee-deep through the tall grasses. Dew lay heavy and sparkling on the eucalypts that fringed the creek banks and slender saplings grew up among the gnarled old box trees that stood on the ridges.

Dana skirted the mustering camp built on a bend of the creek, making a mental note to tell Paddy about the bitter berry that was spreading its squat growth across the entrance to the yard. It was one thing for a steer to race safely under those low branches heavy with foliage and yellow berries, but quite another for a rider in hard pursuit.

Over on the western boundary lay the brigalow, the inpenetrable home of the wallaby and the scrub turkey. Everything there grew wild: lime, pear, the bright green of the wilga, the brooding lawyer vines that draped the glistening silver grey sea of scrub. Out on the flats a mob stood grazing, their sides sleek and red, their down-curving horns showing good breeding. From a vantage point she could see the men going out on a muster. They were divided into two teams of four, set to turn the cattle into the watercourse and gathering in the strays as they went. There were dense patches of timber along the waterways where a cow could stand motionless, unseen by an outriding stockman, and the rogues of the herd knew every one of them. Paddy did not believe in letting the cattle fan out. He had the whole herd under his eye. Her father rarely attended a muster these days. His unique ability did not lie in that direction.

Riding downhill all the way, Dana swung the mare out along the main track back to the homestead, then looked up in surprise at a swirling cloud of dust a half a mile off. She stood up in the stirrups, thoroughly intrigued. It was a car, a late model sedan, metallic green in colour, its chromework flashing in the strong sunlight. Probably a case of mistaken property. They had very few visitors at Mareeba for the very good reason that not many people knew where they were. Sloan Gregory had dropped very completely from public life.

The car slashed out of the sunlight into the shade of the overhanging wattles. Dana swung in beside a clump of paperbarks, sheltering from view. She had no particular desire to be seen. The driver slowed at the turn past the creek, giving her ample time to see inside the vehicle. Recognition came in a split second, and instant pulverising shock. A gigantic Catherine wheel spun round in her head. What was *he* doing here? It just didn't seem possible.

Abruptly the car pulled off the track and up on to a grassy verge. Dana watched dazedly while the driver swung out, lean and rangy, slammed the door to and walked purposefully in her direction, closing in at every stride. Quite obviously he had seen her. She felt incapable of action, wishing desperately to be somewhere else. This man she just could not face. Belatedly she pulled on the reins and turned Sweet Pepper's head about. His voice reached her easily, crisp and authoritative as she just knew it would be. There was a special clarity in the way he bit the words off.

'Hold on there, boy!' Dana ignored him. 'Just a moment, son. I won't eat you.'

She took a deep breath and attempted to move off, but there just wasn't time. He caught her as she tried to mount a bank of spear grass and hauled her out of the saddle. He set her down hard on the ground and jarred her feet. One lean hand slid from the delicate curve of her shoulder to her slender waist and his arrogant gaze travelled over her from her wide-brimmed stetson, framing a deeply feminine face, to the tips of her small, booted feet.

'Not a boy,' he drawled, his eyes leaping with sardonic amusement. 'Good morning, Miss Gregory, not your day for visitors?' he murmured politely.

'Decidedly not!' Dana almost shouted, swallowing hard. One shoulder lifted in obvious irritation. How incredibly stupid she must appear to him! She tried to put on a show and almost succeeded, her voice commendably cool. 'I can't imagine how you know my name, or what you're doing on this property, but I do hope it's a case of mistaken identity.'

He sighed with heavy patience.

'Come now, Dana, you'll have to do better than that. You know me as well as I know you!'

For a second or two she looked like a small replica of her father about to indulge in a fit of temperament. Her amber eyes blazed and the wild apricot colour surged from her cheekbones to the open V of her shirt. He stood regarding her lazily, amused by her reaction and just as obviously expecting it.

'Aren't you being a bit ridiculous? You really should do something about it.'

'Damn it, I will!' Dana shouted, and attempted to vault into the saddle. Her efforts were useless. He simply reached out a long arm and swung her to face him. She stared up at him for a moment, unable to move or think while he looked back at her with the same brilliant stare that had perturbed her so long ago. Then he smiled, his mouth tilting sideways with raffish charm, completely dispelling the dark, sombre look.

'Are you quite finished with the tirade?' he asked equably. 'It's not as if I'm asking you to marry me.'

'I'd have to refuse!' Dana fired at once, annoyed by his facetiousness and his sudden appreciative grin.

'Don't look at me like that, child. You could almost call it positive hatred.'

Dana smouldered in silence. It was strange how much in command of the situation he was, his long lean body relaxed yet curiously alert, so calm and so damned insulting. She fought for a measure of composure, intensely irritated by her own shortcomings in that direction.

'I'm sorry,' she said briskly.

He sketched an ironic bow.

'You don't sound it, but no need to apologise, Miss Gregory. Just try not to do it again.'

Dana almost rose to the bait, then caught the expression in his dark, watchful eyes. She smiled in spite of herself, the sudden revealed whiteness of her teeth especially radiant.

'I'll try if you can tell me very simply what you want.'

'I can and I will. I'd like to speak to your father ... privately.'

Dana raised her chin a fraction. 'I'm afraid that won't be possible.'

'Why? Do you intend to prevent it, my angel?' His black eyebrows lifted.

'Did I say so? Perhaps you would care to tell me what it's about?'

'I would not, you prickly child.'

Dana sighed and brushed her hand against her mouth in a curiously defensive gesture.

'I don't suppose it can do any harm. You might even find time to change your opinion of me,' he smiled.

'In due course, no doubt I shall.' She searched his face for a moment, then added artlessly, 'Besides, I've no choice.'

'True.' His mouth tilted as he watched her turn her head from side to side like a half broken filly.

She looked back at him then, her eyes sparkling with something like temper. Brett's face grew thoughtful.

'You know, I don't care to see such a beautiful girl so belligerent. You won't get a husband that way, Dana. It's too easy to hide your real feelings behind a display of bad temper.'

'Thank you,' she said tartly, 'and you won't get an invitation to the house, always supposing you're about to honour me with your name.'

'Brett Cantrell at your service, ma'am,' he bowed slightly with indolent grace.

'It doesn't mean a thing to me,' Dana said rather rudely, making a small grimace.

He laughed then and turned away from her to the car.

'It will, Dana, it will,' he said briefly, and walked off without so much as a glance to see whether she followed.

Dana swung herself up into the saddle as the car started out along the track. A dull excitement burned along her nerve centres. If she took the short cut across the creek she would beat him back to the house. Brett Cantrell could only mean trouble.

There was salad for lunch, served crisp with a French dressing, locally cured ham, a crusty loaf still warm from the oven and some ripe Brie cheese and tart green apples from the orchard. Dana ate sparingly, for she hadn't any appetite. Her father had produced a light rosé wine with a refreshing tingle, his manner as animated as Dana had seen it for many a long day.

They ate in the cool of the side verandah with country sounds of birds and dogs, distant chugging of machinery and the gentle lowing of the cattle brought in from the outlying ridges. It all added up to peace and contentment, making Dana's feeling of impending upheaval somehow irrelevant.

Her father sat back, contentedly looking across at his guest with obvious approval. Brett Cantrell had introduced himself as a good friend of Colonel Faxon, brought the Colonel's best regards and declared a mutual interest in the breeding of racehorses. Sloan Gregory took to the newcomer on sight and welcomed him in to his home without an instant's hesitation.

'That was a marvellous lunch,' Brett said with approval, glancing across at Dana's down-bent head.

'All in a day's work,' she said crisply. Her father smiled benignly at both of them, quite missing the cross-currents. Dana smoothed the skirt of her tan and gold print. The return to his usual sardonic manner had sparked her anger again. Brett gazed across at the lagoon and commented on its prolific growth of water-lilies, then spoke to his host.

'But I mustn't impose on your hospitality.'

'Heavens, man, you're not thinking of leaving? You must allow me to show you over the property.'

Brett turned his dark clear-cut profile, rewarding the older man with his transforming smile.

'If you're prepared to do that I should be delighted to come along. Perhaps Dana would join us?'

'Of course, of course.' Dana watched the pleasure flood into her father's face. He had taken to the man with a vengeance! Brett Cantrell shot her a sharp sidelong glance as he read her thoughts very accurately. She brushed a hand over her pale shining hair. There was something about him that aroused her suspicions. He knew it, but didn't even have the grace to look embarrassed. Her father was speaking.

'Dana will look after you for a moment while I get that book I was telling you about. It's in my study. I'm sure you'll find it of interest.' He excused himself and went hurriedly out of the room, his step light and purposeful, and Dana was left alone with their visitor.

'What do we do next?' she said very straightly.

'Are you really asking me,' he smiled, 'or is that a rhetorical question?'

She turned her glance away from his mocking dark face and concentrated on a heavy crimson spray of bougainvillea humming with insects all green and gold in the sunlight.

'Obviously you're not the girl to fill every second with scintillating chatter,' he remarked blandly.

She looked at him with open dislike. 'Why do you like baiting me, Mr. Cantrell?'

'Because you rise so beautifully, little one. My apologies, however, if it upsets you.'

'There's got to be a reason,' she said aloud, studying his still dark face.

'Do you always go off at a tangent?' He sounded quite genuinely curious. Dana felt the frustration build in her. This man made her feel extraordinarily young and unworldly, just as he intended her to feel.

He watched her down-bent head with its heavy crescents of dark lashes lying on her cheeks.

'You know, you look quite touchingly young and helpless at the moment and I'm quite sure you're not.' The inflection in his voice unnerved her.

'No, I'm not,' she pointed out hardily, then made a blunt change of topic. 'You and Father are of a height, he'll be able to lend you some gear.'

'That won't be necessary, thank you, Dana. I have some things in the car.'

'How very convenient,' she said with sarcasm, and was rewarded with a hard, speaking look.

'This will be of interest to you, Cantrell.' Her father came back into the room, his glasses perched on his, nose marking a passage with his forefinger.

Brett got up at once and went to look over his shoulder. They were indeed of a similar build, both very tall, very lean, without an ounce of superfluous flesh.

Dana spoke up.

'Mr. Cantrell has his own riding gear, Dad.'

'Good, good,' her father replied absently. 'Come along to the guest room, my dear chap.' The two men walked off, apparently engrossed in blood-lines, leaving Dana to seethe quietly for a reason she was unable to explain to herself.

After the sunlit garden the saddling room seemed very gloomy—a momentary illusion caused by the overhang of the bark roof. Dana ran her hand over her smooth forehead fretfully, as she waited for the men to join her. They had hit it off with a vengeance. She only hoped it wasn't the calm preceding the storm. Yet why should she think that? There was just something about Brett Cantrell she couldn't fathom.

Saddles and gear merged into the dark slab walls. There weren't many horses in, only the quiet working horses; the mustering had only just started. But they all had a trace of Arab blood in them, which was a mark in their favour. Her eye fell on Ghost, the fiddle-headed grey, standing sedately in his stall. The elegant Mr. Cantrell might do well on him—'A nice quiet bit of stuff,' as Paddy would say.

Dana whirled quickly as a long shadow fell across the entrance. Brett ran his eye over her approvingly, bringing the delicate colour to mount beneath her skin. Damn him and his all-seeing eye! He raised one eyebrow rather quizzically at her, then explained:

'Your father will be along in about ten minutes. He's having a yarn to ... Paddy, is it?'

'Paddy it is,' Dana said briefly. She in her turn regarded his impeccable riding-gear with interest. He looked very suave, very urbane in a cream silk shirt and cavalry twill jodhpurs. 'Do you ride much Mr. Cantrell?' she asked innocently.

Brett studied his highly polished boots.

'I can't very well boast, can I? But I just might stick it. Why, have you something in mind for me?'

'Why, yes,' she said brightly, and pointed to old Fiddlehead, who had resumed his peaceable ways after a disinterested look at the visitors. 'Now he's a good walker. I imagine you don't want to be roughed up.' She lifted her long eyes to his face, wide and demure as a child's.

'I trust you're not having a go at me, my girl.' With unflurried ease Brett led the horse out of its stall and reached back for a good, deep-seated saddle. Fiddlehead took the girthing up quietly, but flinched as Brett led him out to the saddling rail.

Dana followed with Sweet Pepper, shading her eyes from the imperious sun. It was a flawless day, the sky a deep peacock blue. Brett swung his mount's head away from the saddling rail and prepared to mount. The grey stood quietly like a sheep while Brett eased his long lithe length into the saddle, then at the first light touch of the heel exploded. Dana stood well back, her heart now thumping wildly! What on earth had she done?

The Ghost laid his ears back, jumped up and clamped his tail down hard between his legs, but he only got a few good bucks in before Brett steadied him, sitting in the saddle as though glued there, not giving the horse its head. He rode beautifully, his shoulders back, the torso swaying hither and thither from his lean hips, now swaying backwards as the grey propped towards the ground. His right hand was held aloft as a counterbalance, free and swinging. It was a perfect example of horsemanship, fluid with easy joints, going with the horse; a world of difference between watching him and the boys rough-riding about the property. Brett depended mostly on balance; there was no perceptible grip, nothing to nullify his fluidity of style. He proved far too good for the Ghost, who had the reputation for grounding anyone foolish enough to mount him. Obviously he had sized up the horse's mental outlook at a glance, assessed correctly the hidden vice.

Gradually the series of flying pigroots petered out until Brett rode the horse round the yard at a walk, at a trot and finally a canter. Dana backed nervously, a fluttering in her stomach.

'You little cat,' Brett said very quietly, dismounting and coming towards her. 'A fair go is a fair go, Dana.' She offered only a token resistance as he reached out for her, purposefully drawing her back into the gloom of the saddling room.

'Well?' She stared up at him defiantly. 'What are you going to do?'

'What I should do is take that strap over there and lay it around you.' There was a flicker in the depths of his near-black eyes.

'You surely wouldn't hit me?' she faltered, unable to loosen his grip upon her.

'I wouldn't be too sure of that. But you'll probably dislike this as much.' One hand jerked her towards him and the other caught the point of her chin in hard, hurting fingers, watching her soft red mouth part in protest and astonishment. He kissed her then, hard and deliberately, provoking an undeniable response. The touch of his mouth and his skin, the scent of him, his long length hard up against her, was bewildering, and frightening. A series of shivers started at the base of her spine and worked up to her neck. The mortified tears sprang to her eyes, an explosive compounding of emotion she was powerless to control.

Brett stood regarding her, his eyes very dark and fathomless.

'What a pity your first kiss had to be so chastening.'

Dana moistened her lower lip with the tip of her tongue, a pallor beneath her pale gold skin.

'I don't want to talk about it.'

'Perhaps not,' a smile twisted his mouth and his face changed. 'As a kiss it left a lot to be desired.'

She moved away from him swiftly with the nervous grace of the young girl. 'Thank you, Mr. Cantrell,' she murmured bitterly, 'but I don't think your own composure is quite real.'

'Now why is it that beautiful girls are so conceited?'

he asked with mock bewilderment. 'One day, young Dana, you'll be quite a woman, but it's a long way off, believe me.' Amber eyes met black velvet, both determined not to yield an inch. Only a few feet separated them, but the gap was charged with tension. Dana felt so shaken, she dared not think about it. She flung up an imperious head and he laughed aloud.

'In your own words, don't be too sure about that,' she said rashly.

'Why, do you intend to prove it to me?' he asked, watching the quick colour mount.

The thought of the possibility made her gasp.

'It's high time we got under way,' she started to say coldly, and walked ahead out into the sunshine.

'Now that's what I call being impulsive!' Brett laughed softly, and followed her determined lead.

—

The afternoon ride was so successful that Brett allowed himself to be induced into catching the mobs as they fed out for the evening. It was the right night for moonlighting, clear and bright with a pearly radiance that lit up the slopes as clearly as broad daylight.

Dana rode out with the men, being quite incapable of sitting at home 'twiddling her thumbs' as Brett had suggested. She watched him riding ahead with her father, swaying easily in the saddle. Paddy in the lead dropped back to point something out to the visitor and Sloan fell back to join his daughter, who was looking surprisingly lost.

'I must say I like Cantrell,' he murmured in a soft telling undertone. 'A very decent chap, knowledgeable too.' This from her father was quite something. 'Just the sort of chap I'd want for you, sweetheart,' he continued in a conversational tone.

'My God!' Dana said violently.

Her father looked across at her in surprise.

'You don't like him?' His voice trailed upwards in astonishment. The idea had simply not occurred to him.

'I don't trust him,' Dana said carefully, and heard in her fancy Brett's voice asking her to suspend her disbelief.

'Good gracious!' her father appeared much struck by this observation and glanced at her warily as though seeing his daughter for the first time as a contrary woman subject to illogical likes and dislikes.

'Why ever not?' he persisted, obviously trying to set her straight. Dana was on the point of telling him where and when she had first seen Brett Cantrell when the mob was sighted. They were in a patch of saplings feeding quietly back towards the scrub.

Paddy swung up a warning hand as he waited for Dana and her father to catch up with them.

'About thirty, boss,' he said laconically. 'A new mob, this one. The big roan in the lead isn't one of ours, I bet my pay packet on it.'

'Well, we have the advantage. They haven't seen us. A short gallop will put us between them and the scrub,' Brett said briefly.

'Right, feller,' Paddy glanced at Brett with increasing respect. 'We'll swing 'em out of the saplings and into the open,' he whispered over his shoulder to Sloan. 'Keep 'em on the run until they're well clear of the scrub. Out in the open, that's where we want them.'

Sloan nodded and immediately they fell into single file, four silent riders, each guiding his mount around branches and stumps that might crack and scrape under hooves and alarm the mob.

At the back of the grazing cattle was the brigalow, a shining silvery canopy under the moon, rising above the dense undergrowth of wilga interlaced with prickly pear. Once in the scrub the stunted bushes between the massed tree trunks could hide the cattle completely.

Brett swung alongside Dana.

'You shouldn't be here, you know that,' he said tersely. 'This is no place for an inexperienced rider.'

Dana almost choked. 'Inexperienced?' she said hotly. 'I'm a darn good rider!'

'Be quiet!' He laid a hard warning hand over hers. 'I meant, you impossible child, for *this* kind of work, though I appreciate your modesty. The ground is criss-crossed with melon holes and fallen branches. You'd better stay here,' he said crisply, and wheeled swiftly after the men, obviously expecting her to do as she was told.

Paddy's shout held an undercurrent of excitement.

'They're off!'

The cattle got into their stride at once, jumping instantly from peaceful grazing to a furious gallop. The men broke fanwise, swinging them in the first headlong rush, and they headed for the open country.

Once the cattle got under way Dana came out of the shadows and rode after them, the night wind tearing through her hair. The horses caught the tension and excitement as they raced over the open ground, avoiding the pitfalls with uncanny presentiment. Paddy swung up in the lead, caught up in the thrill of the chase. They were nearing the yards when the ribbon that tied Dana's hair sailed out on the breeze, unfurling a blonde shaft of silk. She flung her head backwards to clear her face of a heavy silken strand and immediately Sweet Pepper checked, putting her foot in a pothole. Horse and rider came down. They both rolled and were on their feet almost immediately in time to see an old scrub bullock break back towards them. It was a huge old thing with a wickedly sweeping horn spread. Dana stood there panicking, looking frantically for cover.

Brett saw her fall, his breath coming in a hard gasp, as horse and rider righted themselves. When the massive old roan broke from the mob he was ready for it, riding at speed and shouldering it hard, pressing effectively against the solid wall of flesh. The bullock made a few vicious passes until it realised it was wasting its time and energy against this particular rider, then wheeled and thundered after the mob.

'You rash little idiot!' Brett rode in beside her and lifted her into the saddle. He swung her up in front of him and for once Dana had nothing to say for herself. She subsided against him thankfully, her heart beating in painful thuds that seemed to deafen her. Brett's lean arm tightened against her, drawing her hard up against him.

'You can stop trembling now. The hunt's over. If you've got any sense at all, which I doubt, you won't be in another.'

'I was never in any danger,' Dana said faintly, knowing she couldn't have been further from the truth. He ignored her.

'I can believe that, especially with your heart beating wildly against me.'

'Could you ever be wrong about anything?' she said unsteadily.

'I don't propose to be where you're concerned.' He ran a hand over her head and flung the long heavy coil of her hair over her shoulders, his hand biting hard into her slender waist, as they rode back to the yard where the mob were already settled. Sweet Pepper followed them in, causing Paddy to look up in surprise.

'Hello, what's up?'

Sloan straightened up in the saddle after shutting the main gate, echoing Paddy's words.

'Everything all right, Dana ... Brett?'

Dana slipped out of Brett's hard grasp and down on to the ground; strange how unsteady it should feel.

'Sweet Pepper came down in a pothole, Dad. We both took a toss.'

'Good God, dear, to think I never noticed!' Her father moved to her side, quickly dismounting and putting an arm around her.

'Me neither,' Paddy seconded. 'But all's well that ends well. Isn't that right, love?'

'Not in this case, I think, Paddy,' Brett said briefly. 'One of the old scrubbers decided to turn back on her. I wouldn't recommend moonlighting for a woman.'

'You're right, of course,' Sloan said with a slightly guilty air, 'but she's so damn good at it. All the same I think I'll take your advice. The game's up, sweetheart.' He tightened his arm around his daughter.

'Until the next time,' his daughter muttered rebelliously.

'Are you always going to learn the hard way?' Brett came up on her other side, causing her to shrink against her father. The three of them bade goodnight to Paddy, left him to settle the horses, then walked back to the house.

Once inside Dana excused herself, leaving the two men to an easy companionship. In her room with its adjoining bathroom she had a hot shower to ease her now bruised side. She prepared for bed and stood brushing her hair, watching abstractedly the way it flew away with electricity, then settled in a shining bell falling smooth and straight over her shoulders.

There was a tap on the door and she spun quickly, reaching for her ivory peignoir and pushing her arms into it. She tied the ribbons around her narrow waist and walked to the door. It was Brett Cantrell leaning negligently against the door-jamb, not her father. His eyes were black and sparkling and in his hand he held a crystal glass scintillating with a warm topaz liquid. Her father was using the very best for his guest.

'A brandy, young Dana. I think you could do with it.'

'And if I say no?' She fingered the open V-neck of her gown nervously.

'But you won't, will you, Dana? You learn quickly.' His eyes were on her with lazy admiration—the pale shining curtain of hair, the long startled eyes, her clear golden skin innocent of make-up, her soft mouth with its full underlip, caught between her teeth. His eyes lingered on the pulse that beat relentlessly at the base of her throat.

'Go on, drink it,' he ordered, 'I won't go until you do, and that's what you want, isn't it?'

'For you to go, certainly,' Dana said recklessly, and tossed off the contents, almost but not quite gagging on it.

He smiled then, a real smile that lit his eyes and tilted his mouth in such a devastating fashion.

'Go to bed, child. You'll need a good night's sleep if you're to get through tomorrow.'

She looked up quickly directly to meet his gaze with her own. 'What on earth do you mean?' she asked.

'Why, nothing, my pet,' he murmured sardonically,

not moving his eyes from hers. She coloured delicately and he smiled a little. 'Until tomorrow, then, Miss Gregory.' He moved away from the door, bidding her goodnight with mock politeness.

Dana stood quite still for a few extra moments, wondering what on earth he was up to.

CHAPTER THREE

THERE was complete silence at the breakfast table and an overriding consternation. Sloan Gregory sat very straight in his chair and regarded his guest with frosty blue eyes.

'But what could have persuaded you to leave it until now to tell me about this, Cantrell?'

His guest returned his gaze very directly.

'Thinking back on it, would you have suggested I tell you the very first day?'

'Perhaps not,' the older man conceded, 'but I don't mind telling you, I'm disappointed in you, bitterly disappointed. Had I known at the outset that you had the controlling interest in Rankine Stud it would have altered matters considerably. I trusted you completely, my boy.'

Brett was a little pale under his teak tan.

'To be fair, did I tell you anything that was untrue?'

'It's what you didn't tell us,' Dana burst out fiercely.

'Keep out of this, Dana,' Brett said warningly.

'Yes, keep out of this,' her father seconded, bearing out her contention that men invariably stick together. Brett lent an elbow on the table, bringing to bear the full weight of his sharp powers of persuasion. His penetrating gaze held Sloan's.

'I'll admit I was influenced by Tod's opinions. And why not? I'd been overseas for six years, the last three of them spent in the States. You know yourself Tod was a man of unfailing integrity. His only mistake was in thinking you were not. Unfortunately he never got the chance to discover differently. His heart was always tricky. Your name and reputation was only hearsay. I had no personal knowledge of you then. I'll tell you now, if it matters at all, that I'm quite convinced you're a man to be depended upon implicitly.'

A flush stained Sloan Gregory's strong cheekbones.

'I suppose I should thank you for that, but no, Cantrell, no. My answer is most definitely no, no matter how good you say the horse is, or rather potentially good in the right hands. Surely you can find another trainer if you're not satisfied with Logan?'

Brett shrugged impatiently. 'Of course I can, the lot if I want them, but I want the best, and that's you. With you on my side I can bring the Cup back to the Rankine Stud. Whatever happened to the Prince, and I have my theories on that, I'm convinced you bear no blame in the matter.'

Sloan sighed heavily and passed a weary hand across his eyes.

'No, Brett. No,' he said less vehemently, 'I can't back down now, I tell you.'

'Oh, be damned!' Brett flung himself up from the table impatiently. 'It took me long enough to find you, God knows. If I hadn't run into Faxon...' He let that trail off, then swung back on them. 'I'm going into town for the night. *One* night only, understand. Try and see it my way. You're no cattleman. Your genius lies in training thoroughbreds and I've got one on my hands that needs your attention. Its sire is the Prince, if that's any inducement.' Brett leant down and grasped Dana's wrist, hauling her up to him. 'Dana will see me out,' he said in a tone that brooked no opposition.

Sloan watched almost helplessly while his visitor

stalked out of the room with his daughter pulling against him. His face held a mixture of regret and longing—expressions his daughter had come to know well.

In the sunshine Brett pulled Dana along with him to where the car was parked in the shade of the acacias.

'Try and make your father see sense,' he ordered imperiously.

'My God, but you've got the arrogance of the devil himself!' she burst out.

He turned on her then, pushing up her chin with hurting fingers.

'*I* have? Let me tell you, you've got more than your share of it, my lady.' His black eyes sparkled dangerously. 'Your father is the best trainer in the country, that is to say one of the best in the world, do you understand? What do you want him to do? Go to seed in the bush? Trying to live out his life on a property he's only halfhearted about? It's not good enough, I tell you.'

'Oh, why don't you go to the devil?' she said heatedly, disliking the picture he was painting. It was far too accurate.

'Don't try me too far, little one,' he bit out, his teeth clenched and his eyes sparkling with anger. 'You have considerable influence with your father. Try to use it wisely. I want him at the Stud, it's in his own best interests. You might remember I usually get my way.'

'Not always, Mr. Cantrell,' she said with pleasurable emphasis.

Brett held her face between his hands and shook her while her head lolled on her slender neck.

'Always, Dana,' he stressed. 'Try to remember it. It will make for an easier life.' He released her then, leaving her rocking on her heels while he went to the car, opening the door and slamming it hard in an excess of temper, after him. 'Until tonight,' he said with emphasis, and swung the car out on to the drive.

Dana looked after him in perplexity. He was right, of course. In her way her father was hiding out. He was, as he admitted on odd occasions, sensitive and proud to a fault. It only needed a word from her to spring the scales in Brett Cantrell's favour. But why should she do it? Didn't he always get his own way? she reflected bitterly.

She walked back to the house and found her father still in his chair, obviously waiting for her to rejoin him.

'Well, what do you think of that?' he asked her, examining her face closely.

'I'm not surprised at all.' Dana pulled her chair closer to her father. 'I don't imagine Mr. Brett Cantrell ever does anything without a motive.'

'Yet he's right, isn't he? And he is a business man.' Perversely her father now began to defend their departed guest. 'Getting to know and like him has clouded matters a bit.'

'Oh, Dad!' Dana sighed impatiently. 'You can't pull a man in two, and that's what's happening to you. It's in your blood ... you only come alive when you're around your beloved horses. We acted too impulsively. Perhaps we should have stayed. Others ride out the storm if they have to.'

For some reason her father became annoyed with this statement and got up from the table in a temper. It seemed it was the morning for them.

'We'll say no more about it,' he announced very sharply for him, and withdrew from the room leaving

Dana to think dark thoughts about Mr. Brett Cantrell and his famous Rankine Stud.

It was strange, though, how few people knew Tod Rankine had another nephew other than the well-known playboy and man-about-town, Jeff Rankine. Briefly Dana wondered how he had taken the news that his uncle's property had passed largely into the hands of his sister's only child, a dark horse if ever there was. After a while she got up from the table and began to rearrange all the furniture, something she always did when perturbed.

Rattling into town in the old utility, Dana wondered for perhaps the hundredth time if now she had embarked upon her course she was really doing the right thing. Her father had roamed around restlessly all day, unable to settle to anything, and finally retired early complaining of a violent headache.

Dana's mind was made up. She took particular care with her appearance that evening, if only to give her confidence, she told herself. The short bronze crêpe was new and threw a glow over her skin, pointing up the colour of her hair and eyes. If her father couldn't or wouldn't come to a decision, she would do it for him. She thought of her own dear mother. She had been barely thirteen when her mother died, yet she remembered very clearly how the beautiful Abby had handled her temperamental husband, unobtrusively pointing the way for him until all the major decisions seemed to be his alone and the minor ones hers entirely.

Dana blinked back the tears that always sprang to her eyes when she thought of her mother. Ah well, she was a very poor substitute, but she would do her best.

'Fools rush in where angels fear to tread'—the words of the old song ran through her head and immediately her mood brightened. She made it into the town in record time, parking outside the one and only hotel. She felt enormously elated suddenly, as though she had taken a giant step in the right direction. At this rate she would have her father back where he belonged in no time. Her optimism carried her forward almost gaily to the dimly lit entrance, and then she came up short. A reception desk, a notice board covered with coloured posters, a rack of keys, another of letters, a clerk in an off-white shirt leaning back lackadaisically in his swivel chair met her momentarily dazzled eyes. The clerk stood up at once as he felt her eyes on him, and smiled widely in markedly false bonhomie. As she stepped further into the light he recognised her.

'Good evening, Miss Gregory.' There was an insinuating softness in his voice that she found rather unpleasant. It dropped to a confidential level. 'Can I help you?'

'Yes,' Dana said at once, trying not to sound unpleasant herself. 'The number of Mr. Brett Cantrell's room, please?'

The clerk blinked for a moment, then smiled his disagreeable smile again.

'Number ten, Miss Gregory.' He continued to smile knowingly and watched her long golden legs flash away from him. That Dana Gregory was a 'terrific sort' in his opinion, but much too stuck-up for his liking. The thought crossed his mind to give that Cantrell chap a buzz, but he had second thoughts about it. Now *he* was just the type to punch you in the nose if you interfered in his affairs.

Dana stood outside number ten, her heart beating

uncomfortably. She swallowed on a dry throat, then tapped on the door and waited for his relaxed and indifferent 'Come in'.

She opened the door and saw him at once, long and lean, lounging on the bed looking over the top of a current bestseller. He swung his legs down and came to attention, throwing the book on the bed.

'Well, well,' he said almost gently. His eyes took in her smooth blonde perfection, then he leaned back against the window and folded his arms, waiting for her to make the first move.

'You're not making it easy,' Dana said nervously, and backed a fraction. He came away from the window and walked over to her, reaching out to shut the door firmly behind her.

'You bring out the worst in me, do you know that, Dana?' He turned back to her and his eyes were wickedly black. She changed places with him quickly and went to lean against the window, putting some distance between them.

'Say your piece, Dana,' he prompted, observing her actions with interest.

She came straight to the point without further preamble.

'You win, Mr. Cantrell. Father isn't happy, hasn't been since two-forty-five on the first Tuesday of November three years ago, to be exact. He'll join you whenever you're ready for him.'

'And why can't he tell me all this?' Brett was watching her closely.

'He doesn't know yet,' Dana answered with simple honesty.

He laughed outright.

'Dana, Dana, and to think I thought you a helpless

little thing! Or did I?' His black eyes openly mocked her.

'I don't give a damn what you think of me,' she said unsteadily, unstrung as she always was in his presence. 'You'll be getting your way, that's the main thing,' she flashed back at him with spirit, 'but don't ever ask me to like you, Mr. Cantrell. I just couldn't do it.'

He came a step nearer, making her retreat in the strangest panic.

'Did I ever say I wanted you to like me, you conceited child? I'd much rather you hated me, for that matter.'

She turned her head swiftly from his overbright glance. 'In that case, your worries are over!'

His laugh floated to her ears, low and resonant. She made to move past him, but he caught her wrist, holding her still.

'How did you get here?'

'In the ute, of course.'

His eyebrows came together. 'Well, you're not going back in it.'

'Why ever not?' Dana asked in astonishment. 'The worst I could do is hit a wallaby.'

He reached over for his jacket and shouldered into it. 'I'll run you back.'

'And how do you propose to get back, Mr. Cantrell? Walk?' she said sweetly.

'You can stop the backchat,' he said very crisply, and flicked off the overhead light. They stood for a moment in total darkness, brittle with tension, until Dana spoke his name in a tentative husky whisper ... 'Brett?'

He laughed suddenly and she felt intensely foolish. He opened the door and light flooded into the room.

'It was worth it to stop you calling me Mr. Cantrell.'

She glanced up at his dark profile but he was looking straight ahead, his mind on other things. When they got downstairs Brett walked over and had a word with the desk clerk, who was all eyes and ears.

'Whatever did you say to him?' Dana asked when they were out on the pavement.

'Questions, questions! What a formidable young woman you are, Dana. I merely asked him to run the ute out and I'll drive him back, God help me. It won't be any loss to the community if he runs off the track.'

'And I will?' She glanced up at him, her long amber eyes sparkling.

'Can you doubt it?' he asked with charming mockery, his smile almost inducing her to change her mind about him.

Inside the hotel the desk clerk pocketed his ten dollars cheerfully. That Cantrell wasn't a bad bloke after all, and *she* was absolutely gorgeous when she smiled.

CHAPTER FOUR

RANKINE STUD was set in eight hundred acres of lush, undulating grasslands an hour's drive from Melbourne, one of the most beautiful cities in the world and the heart of Australia's art, finance and industry.

The Stud, one of the finest breeding and racing establishments in the country, was entirely self-contained, from starting stalls to farrier's workshops. The stabling for the mares and the stallions was on the grand scale and dozens of loose-boxes were provided for the yearlings. Shelter boxes stood in everyone of the forty thickly grassed paddocks permanently watered by the river nearby.

The house itself, a mansion, was set in six acres of magnificent grounds and often appeared in the glossy magazines under the caption 'One of our finest examples of Colonial architecture'.

John Rankine, who had come out from England in the mid-1800s, was a man of strong individuality and determination, a splendid horseman, and a consummate judge of horseflesh. His great affection for horses had led to an interest in training which in turn progressed from an absorbing hobby to full-time obsession. It was he who built the big house and formed the Rankine Stud which his eldest son, Tod, was to bring to outstanding eminence.

Tod Rankine, who had taken a degree in economics, rather drifted into the world of the thoroughbred. He loved his father's horses and spent all his available time schooling his own horses on his father's property, but he had come to regard the Stud as a perilous business venture. When his father died leaving it to him, he determined to make a success of it, purely as a sideline, with such staggering results that his death automatically closed a page of racing history.

Silent as he was on all family and racing matters except to his closest friends, no one connected with the Turf expected that the property would go to any other than his nephew, Jeffrey Rankine, a good judge of horses, admittedly, but unlike his uncle a heavy gambler and well-known man about town.

Tod Rankine's death, received with widespread regret, triggered off almost as much regret when the name of his successor was released to the Press—Brett Cantrell, an unknown name in the racing world. Described by some notable authorities as too young and too inexperienced to take over such an outstanding establishment, he proved within three years that he had the eye, the judgment, and the business brain to stay on the top in the tough racing world, leaving his former detractors strangely silent.

The Rankine Stud was still reaping rich rewards in the Eastern States, but the coveted Melbourne Cup had eluded its owner—an unsatisfactory result for a man like Brett Cantrell. To win a Melbourne Cup was the aspiration of every owner, trainer and jockey in the country. It was Brett Cantrell's aspiration, and he went out after what he wanted in life and usually got it.

Driving through the massive black wrought-iron gates that led up to the house, Dana thought it was not quite as she remembered it. It was better. Her observant eye picked up numerous minor changes that enhanced an already beautiful home. Superfluous details had been removed and the porches had been redesigned while still retaining the essential charm of a gracious old home. Excitement gripped her as she gazed up at the stately white-columned mansion. She had only been in it once; Tod Rankine had always visited her father's establishment, not the other way round.

The chauffeur-driven limousine cruised up the circular gravelled drive and swept to a halt at the base of the stairs, four wide, shallow marble steps, leading to the house. Busy with her thoughts, Dana started slightly when her father spoke to her.

'Well, this is it, dear. The start of a long happy association ... we hope.'

She smiled at him encouragingly as he helped her out of the car. The chauffeur touched a finger to his hat and drove off, taking their luggage around to the service lift. So far no one was in sight, but as they mounted the steps the door opened and an attractive fair-headed man moved towards them.

'I see you made it,' he said somewhat superfluously.

Sloan Gregory extended his hand.

'Nice to be here. How are you, Jeff? I don't think you've met my daughter, Dana?'

'Most certainly not.' Jeffrey Rankine looked her over with obvious approval. 'And a beauty too.'

'You flatter me, Mr. Rankine,' Dana murmured, and gave him her hand. He held it warmly.

'Truth is not flattery, my dear Dana.' The hand was transferred to her shoulders as he drew her into the house. His manner was warm—too warm, Dana thought uncomfortably.

'Welcome to the ancestral home. Not my idea of one, too big to be sensible.' He turned to smile at Sloan, giving Dana the opportunity to slip nimbly out of grasp. 'Brett, dear boy, has had to make a rush trip to Sydney ... lovely place, but he left me to do the honours.'

A tall dark-haired young woman came down the stairway in time to hear his last sentence. There was a cold surprise on her face that Dana and her father found offensive.

'Ah, Margot darling, come and meet our guests.' He turned his dark blond head with its lighter sun-streaks.

For acknowledgment the young woman's eyebrows shot up, but she condescended to come over to them. She was certainly good-looking with crisp, blue-black hair, and an oval patrician face out of which looked two of the brightest and chilliest blue eyes Dana had ever seen.

Jeff was smiling.

'Sloan, Dana, I'd like you to meet my wife. These are the Gregorys, darling, Brett's guests.' He spaced his words evenly, giving them time to sink in.

'Yes, of course,' Margot murmured, her blue eyes taking on a cold appraising expression.

By this time Jeff was looking hard, obviously trying to whip some life into her, but she decided to confound him and cut the encounter short.

'I'd expect you'd like to see your rooms,' she said, boredom coming back into her face. 'Jeff will show you. I expect I'll see you at dinner.' She turned away and walked to one of the smaller rooms that led off the entrance hallway.

'Charming girl, my wife,' Jeff muttered as she disappeared, a frankly cynical expression crossing her face. 'But she is good-looking—that's the only explanation I can offer.'

Dana and her father avoided looking at one another. It would keep until later.

'Well, she's got a point anyway.' Jeff brightened and took Dana's arm again. 'I expect you would like to see your rooms ... settle in before dinner.' He gave them a brilliant smile. 'With any luck Brett won't—correction, will—be back this evening.'

He led them through to the west wing along wide marble-floored galleries, punctuated with expansive views of the landscaped grounds. Dana glanced briefly at exotic benches and chests, sculptures and pictures, all facing the windowed walls. She determined at her leisure to study them.

Jeff was being very affable, whether to make up for his wife's shortcomings or whether it was part and parcel of the man, neither could tell. He saw them to their adjoining suites, reminding them that dinner was at seven, but to come down for drinks a good half hour before that. The last was accompanied by another of his flashing smiles.

Dana waited for her father to come back into her room, saving her reactions for mutual evaluation.

'My God, there's a turn-up for the book!' Sloan Gregory put his head around the door and shut it carefully behind them. 'Did you ever?'

'Never,' Dana said firmly.

Her father came right into the room, whistling appreciatively at the decor.

'What Paddy would call "a bit of all right".' He sat down on the bed and traced a finger over the raised pattern of the quilted bedspread.

'What a lovely time we'll all have together.' Dana lent down and gave him a hug. 'I suppose you could charitably describe her as a bitch.'

'Definitely. I didn't even know Jeff was married.'

'Well, he knows,' Dana said with certainty. 'We might as well think of other accommodation, Dad. Of course we don't know the woman, but I feel our Margot dislikes us and she's not a woman to make a big secret of it.'

'No,' her father laughed quietly, his mouth wry with amusement. 'Oh well, Mareeba's always there with Paddy in charge. Still, Brett's our man, and I for one like and trust him.'

'Umm,' Dana contributed, and walked across and looked out of the window at the beautiful sweep of lawn, the magnificent pin-oaks standing against the last rays of the sun. Evening was pressing in and a purple dusk invading the sky.

'I can't see him putting up with her,' she observed feelingly.

'Who, Brett?'

'Who else?' Dana turned back from the window. 'He's quite a different proposition from his cousin. I can just see him firing a woman out of the nearest window if she got on his nerves!'

'Not a bad idea if you're game,' her father smiled, and looked around the high-ceilinged room. 'This is a wonderful old house, isn't it? Must have quite a few stories to tell. From the little I know of Jeff Rankine Tod made the only possible will. With Brett the stud is at least assured of a future.'

Dana listened to her father's championship of their host in a speaking silence. She walked backwards and forwards, putting her things away with a remarkable economy of movement.

'My goodness, you're efficient,' her father broke off to redirect his praises.

'That's my strong point—efficiency. I feel sure Mr. Brett Cantrell will set great store by it.'

Sloan Gregory hoped he didn't look as surprised as he felt. This antagonism Dana felt for Brett Cantrell was quite beyond his understanding. For what reason he wasn't quite sure, he would have trusted the man with his life, as he was in a sense doing.

'I'm sure you'll come to see Brett differently,' he said very gravely.

'Now there's a hope!' Dana spoke with such an air of disbelief that her father burst out laughing, the corners of his eyes crinkling. He got up from the bed and patted her cheek. 'Well, failing that I think I'll have forty winks before dinner. I'm rather tired.'

Dana smiled at him and took a few dancing steps in front of him.

'Won't you come into my parlour...' she began, and waved her hand towards the door and back again with a flourish.

Her father laughed. 'There's no need to be scared. We'll make out.'

Dana managed a faint grin. 'Who said anything about being scared? See you later, Dad. I might have a rest myself.'

Her father went out of the room, leaving her staring at the closed door. 'Said the spider to the fly,' she continued to herself solemnly, then sat down on her bed to contemplate her room.

If nothing else it was decidedly comforting. Flower prints in heavy gold frames hung above two deep upholstered armchairs that flanked the fireplace, with a long low table in between. The walls were covered in an ivory, gold-flecked wallpaper, the quilted headboard of the bed was gold, matching the ottoman at its foot. The windows were draped in ivory with swag valances of the same topaz as the deeply piled rug in the centre of the room. It might almost have been planned for her. She lay back on the huge antique bed, staring up at its tentlike canopy. Gradually without realising it she drifted off into a light sleep. Her father wasn't the only one who was tired.

A tap on the door and her father's voice aroused her. She blinked sleepily and switched on the bedside lamp.

'Hello, I'm awake.'

'I'll be going down in about fifteen minutes, dear.'

'Good, Dad, I'll be there.'

Dana lay a moment longer, then showered and dressed, choosing a floating chiffon dress of sugar-spun fineness a few shades darker than her eyes. She noted with approval that the shadow of fatigue had vanished from under her eyes. In fact she had never looked better. The night air blowing through the open windows was warm and heavy with the white-starred scent of jasmine.

When she went out into the hallway her father was coming out of his room. His eyes lit up at once with parental pride, telling her very plainly that she was a credit to him.

'That's a pretty dress, dear—all drifting grace. You look like my darling Abby.'

Dana glanced down at her frock, biting her lip. 'I dozed off, Dad, would you believe it!'

'Better than lying awake thinking about things,' he observed shrewdly. 'Well, let's get it over with.'

Dana laughed and slipped a hand through the curve of his arm as they walked down the long carpeted hallway.

'We might as well spy out the land as we go,' she

said, looking down the stairs.

'That won't be necessary. I hope to have the pleasure of showing you over the house myself.' Brett Cantrell came up behind them from the other end of the hallway. Dana and her father turned in an instant, the one displaying open pleasure, the other considerable reserve.

He looked as elegant as only a tall man can look in evening clothes, his ruffled white shirt throwing his teak tan into stunning relief. Brett Cantrell was being very smooth, very pleasant, serenely assured, apologising for his necessary absence. He was also just a little too good to be true, Dana thought critically, making a point of not meeting the brilliant dark gaze.

He accompanied them to the living room pointing out this and that antique on the way and promising them a closer look at it later. Margot and Jeff Rankine were already there. They were both subdued, but looked up with automatic civility. Civility vanished when Margot looked over Dana's head to Brett standing just behind her shoulder. A curious expression flickered across her face, to be replaced by a glow in the shocking blue eyes.

'You came at the right time, Brett. Jeff and I were just getting to the tedious stage,' she said gaily, displaying an animation neither Dana or her father would have given her credit for. One long pale hand ran along the edge of her chair with nervous impatience.

'And so early in the evening, Margot,' Brett said lightly, and turned to his cousin, thanking him for looking after his guests.

'A pleasure, old son,' Jeff responded, and glanced over at the bar at one end of the room. 'How about giving me your orders?'

The two men accepted a Scotch and water, while Dana sipped at a dry Martini, feeling very sophisticated. Surprisingly Margot patted the place beside her.

'Come sit beside me.' She looked across at the younger girl with a show of the womenfolk sticking together. Dana hesitated for a fraction of a second, then crossed to the long divan, studiously hiding her inner reluctance.

'I do like your dress,' Margot said languidly. 'It's quite lovely.' Her eyes were taking in the details of the dress, assessing its cost with obvious surprise.

Dana bowed her head. 'Thank you. Your own is a model, isn't it?'

'Of course,' Margot said complacently, patting the heavy silk. She watched the men move off to the bar with something like relief. Her voice dropped to a low conversational note.

'I do hope you appreciate what Brett is doing for you and your father. Just like Brett to attempt it.'

'I beg your pardon?' Dana spoke as coldly as the other girl.

'Don't play the injured innocent with me. It's a straight case of rehabilitation, isn't it? I do know something of your history.' Margot dropped any pretence at civility, her dislike very obvious. Dana felt her heart begin to beat very fast.

'You may know some of our history, but you're obviously in ignorance of the facts.'

Margot laughed shortly. 'Don't they all say that?'

Dana looked straight at her, her eyes very clear, very amber.

'Let me give you a piece of gratuitous advice, Mrs. Rankine. Don't criticise my father to me. It's liable to make me see red.'

Margot was silent, digesting this, then she smiled rather unpleasantly.

'How dutiful! An admirable characteristic, I'm sure, but not one I greatly admire.' Her eyes were ice blue, cold and calculating.

Dana stood up without any outward show of haste.

'You'll excuse me, won't you? I feel the sudden need for fresh air.'

A flush stained Margot's cheeks as Dana turned away, hoping her own colour had not risen, though she knew her eyes would be brighter than usual.

Brett separated himself from the men and came towards her, looking down at her intently.

'How are you, Dana?' His voice was quiet, almost gentle, but she didn't trust his gentleness.

'Very well, thank you, Mr. Cantrell.'

His eyes were fixed on her face and she felt her mouth tremble.

'You'll have to convince me of that. You look decidedly keyed up at the moment.'

'I assure you I'm not,' she said untruthfully, thinking it was no concern of his if she was. He was of no importance to her, she told herself fiercely, and knew in an instant how utterly untrue it was.

'Relax, little one,' Brett said quietly. 'You're too highly strung.' He took hold of her elbow in a steadying grip and turned to invite the others in to dinner. Behind him Margot's eyes met hers with cold distaste and an over-riding resentment. It's quite possible she'll make a cardboard replica of me and stick pins in it, Dana thought a shade hysterically. She moved closer to Brett without being aware of it. He glanced down at her smooth blonde head gleaming like polished silk under the lights, his eyes very dark and watchful.

Dana looked up then and caught his expression. It was an instant of sudden awareness. She felt she could do almost anything. There seemed to be countless things she wanted to say. The room hushed and her vision was blocked by a sombre dark face, still and exciting.

'How often does this kind of thing happen?' Jeff loomed up behind them, a flicker of awakening curiosity in his eyes.

'Not often enough.' Brett's expression changed to one of smooth sociability. 'Let's go in to dinner, shall we?'

Jeff continued to look at them with mild surprise, his wife with a twist of near-hatred.

All through dinner Dana tried to sit relaxedly against the tension that was gathering. She looked over at Brett, his sleek dark head, dark eyes, lean distinctive elegance, and looked away again. Jeff and her father were talking briefly together and Margot was holding her wine-glass with an all-absorbing interest. Dana heard the softened tone, the extra-sensitive awareness in Margot's voice as she spoke to him. There was no possible doubt, Margot Rankine was strongly attracted to the wrong man. Whatever she felt for her husband, it palled into significance beside what she did, or could, feel for his cousin. An explosive set-up! Dana wondered rather vehemently if the attraction was mutual and felt inexplicably repelled by the idea.

The soufflé passed and then coffee, before she stole another glance at Brett from under her heavy dark lashes, only to find his eyes directly upon her. She looked back at him defiantly, all her original distrust of him bubbling back. Of course it was mutual! Even if she didn't care for him herself there was something about him, a subtle sexuality that most women would instantly recognise and find too heady to resist. His expression hardened as he gauged the train of her thoughts correctly. Brilliant accusation flashed out of her eyes. Beside him Margot had thawed into exquisite complacency, her eyes glowing secretly. Dana stood up suddenly, feeling the need for physical action. Brett stood up too and began to move towards her.

'I find your eagerness to examine my first editions quite gratifying, Dana.'

Margot looked blank, her rarefied air once more in evidence.

'First editions?' she echoed, looking very closely at both of them.

'It's not as funny as it sounds,' Dana said cryptically, and tensed up as Brett took her elbow, painfully, though she made no sign of it.

'Well, come on, now.' He looked back at the others, turning on the charm. 'You'll excuse us for a few moments, won't you? I promise to show Dana some valuable first editions I've managed to pick up in my travels.'

Her father looked pleased but nonplussed.

'Go along by all means, dear. Jeff is just bringing me up to date on some racing matters.'

'I really don't ...' Margot started to say, and subsided under the malicious gaze her husband turned upon her.

Brett moved swiftly, then, almost pushing her through to his study that led off the original double parlours. It looked just like him—individual, streamlined, organised for work. The colour scheme was muted, but the room abounded in warm textures from the rugged stone wall, the shaggy grey carpet, and grey velvet armchairs to the brilliant accent of a long zebra-upholstered divan. A whole wall of books beautifully bound sprang to life that might easily contain any number of rare books. Dana glanced at him briefly, then away again, involuntarily shielding her eyes from the dark mastery of this impossible stranger.

'This doesn't make sense.'

'Neither does your behaviour,' he bit out, 'transparent as it may be.'

'If it comes to that, what about your own?' Her voice trailed off, heavy with innuendo.

Brett's eyes snapped dangerously. 'There are some things I'll take from you, Dana, and some I won't.'

'You're very lordly, aren't you?' She tilted her smooth pale head away from him.

'I've never thought about it. But I do know you have to get over the top of women, the spirited ones especially.'

'You sound very experienced.'

'Even if I wasn't I'd be getting plenty of it with you around.'

'I can't wait!'

He turned on her then, grasping the soft flesh of her upper arms.

'Listen, you irritating little devil! You're going to try to settle down here. You love your father, don't you? Forget about me. Concentrate on him.'

'I don't understand you.' Nervously she twisted away from him, keeping her eyes down.

'I think you do. You're just going to beat helplessly around for a while. Isn't that it?'

'You're far too involved for me, Mr. Cantrell,' she flared sarcastically, and was caught and then held against him in a hard strong grasp. She lost her composure then and her feeling of equality. She struggled helplessly against his grip, heard her own voice saying:

'You're hurting me, Brett!' Her fear of him showed in her voice and he released her at once.

'Not half as much as I'd like to.' His voice was hard and cold. 'Don't trade on your sex too much, little one, you might be in for some surprises.'

Dana rallied then, her chin lifting. 'You make me tremble!'

'I could do very easily. For all your bravado you're only an innocent, unaware of your own power.'

'Power—me?' Dana looked incredulous.

Brett frowned, his face dark and remote.

'All beautiful women wield a quite terrifying power, Dana. You're very beautiful, even if you're a totally unlikeable brat.'

She looked startled.

'I suppose I am. Around you, anyway.'

'And why is that, do you suppose?' he asked with extreme sarcasm.

She lost her temper then and shouted at him.

'How the hell should I know? You're a totally unlikeable, self-opinionated, self-centred, overbearing, sadistic...'

'Shut up!' he said, and took her shoulders in his now familiar hard grip shaking her so that her head snapped. Dana took a deep shuddering breath. Brett's hand was at the back of her head now, almost caressing the nape.

'All right, take it easy now,' he said roughly. 'Do you suppose we can behave like two ordinary civilised people?' His grip was still firm but warmer, now more comforting than frightening.

'No, I'm afraid not,' Dana said dazedly, then almost

against her will raised her head, watching in fear and fascination his dark head come down to her.

'You silly child.' His voice was quiet, hardly more than a murmur.

A knock at the door burst the bubble, separating them in an instant. Brett reached over her head and pulled down a little book with a faded blue cover.

'Look,' he said, his voice sounding crisp and loud to her ears, 'this is quite unusual.'

Dana pulled herself together, trying to read the find gold print on the cover. But it was no use. Her head was swimming sickeningly.

Margot stood inside the doorway, watching them intently. Brett let a few significant seconds go by, then he turned very casually.

'Yes, Margot?'

'I wish you'd asked me to see those first editions, Brett. How is it you never have?' She looked bewildered, excited, sinking lower into the quicksand of his attraction for her. Does he know it? Dana thought wearily. Who was he to talk of power?

'I'd be delighted to, Margot,' Brett said calmly, the smooth mask settling over his face.

'I just didn't realise you'd be interested.'

'In that case you'll excuse me,' Dana murmured a shade incoherently, and moved across the room with a swift unconscious grace.

Outside in the hallway she wondered rather wildly how Brett could possibly get over the hurdle of producing rare books from the thin air. Even for him that might prove difficult.

CHAPTER FIVE

PRINCE GAUNTLETT was a beautifully balanced black horse of spectacular beauty, standing just over sixteen hands. His sire was the highly credentialled Prince Akura and his dam the fiery and unpredictable Storm Queen whose moodiness caused her withdrawal from racing after she had proved her quality by winning a string of two-year-old races in brilliant competition.

Dana leaned against the white rails of the practice yard watching Brett and her father discussing the stallion's points. One thing was evident: it had spirit, perhaps an excess of it.

'Good head, plenty of courage and intelligence there, deep shoulders, plenty of room behind the saddle, powerful hindquarters.'

They stood with their arms leaning on the rails, watching. The big black showing his beautiful swaying walk as the stable boy rode him around.

'Effortless at his top.' Brett turned to the older man, now completely engrossed in the horse. 'Logan wanted to geld him, quieten him down. He's not too popular with the boys, you know. Too cantankerous, too much biting and kicking.'

'Umm.' Sloan Gregory digested this in silence. He was no great admirer of Logan. His methods were too harsh, in his opinion, but he did get results providing the horse could take it. 'How is he at the track?'

'Imperturbable. It's his off-track performances that have me worried. You know Storm Queen's history, of course. Yet in the right hands he'll make a fabulous racehorse. I'm convinced of it.' Brett hit the fence as he spoke and the stallion reared high on his powerful hind legs. His diminutive rider, a sandy-haired lad of about fifteen, sat him with confidence, evidently used to his mount's quirks of temperament.

Brett glanced away from the stallion. 'He'll stroll away when he feels like it with plenty in reserve. But when he doesn't——!' He gestured expressively, leaving Sloan to draw his own conclusions. 'He's too unstable. It's up to you to ease him into a settling programme. Handle him your way without interference. One thing, he's had all the advantages of slow, careful work. He's been nursed along quietly. There is a top-quality stayer, if we can only stabilise him.'

Sloan nodded agreement. 'Patience is something you have to have in unlimited quantities when you're dealing with racehorses. There's nothing quite like having a promising horse realise his potential. From the looks of the Prince I'm inclined to agree with you.' He turned to his daughter. 'What about you, darling?'

Dana watched the sun strike off the glistening ebony coat of the Prince. 'A really outstanding horse always has plenty of spirit, hasn't he, Dad? He does seem a bit cantankerous, though.'

For no apparent reason Brett laughed. Dana looked across at him sharply, but he assumed a mock gravity.

'You were saying, Miss Gregory?'

'You think my opinion of little consequence, Mr. Cantrell?'

'Dana darling!' Her father watched the signs of a flare up of temperament. His daughter's long amber eyes were flashing bright, the warm colour racing into her flawless face. She reminded him vividly of Abby in the early days when their love had been so tempestuous. He sighed deeply stirred out of the present into the rapturous past.

'Now who's cantankerous?' Brett said blandly. 'Dana, Dana,' he said her name as though it were a caress.

Dana looked at him speechlessly, caring nothing for yesterday, today or tomorrow. Her physical response to him caught at her breath, set her pulses throbbing. It was something to be clamped down on. She lifted her face and took a deep breath.

'Well, now, it might be best if I leave you two authorities to it,' she said ironically. 'I'm sure there's some woman's work I can turn my hand to. Dusting perhaps, all those knick-knacks.' She moved away quickly, dreamlike, hearing Brett's voice saying:

'Do take the short cut.' The laugh in his voice was apparent. She stumbled a little in her hurry and made quite a creditable recovery. Damn Brett Cantrell and his ascendancy over her! For the first time in her life she felt disgruntled with her father. Why was it that men invariably stuck together?

Jeff Rankine was in the hallway running through the morning's mail. His hazel eyes were very bright as he looked at Dana with slow attention.

'How goes it, Golden Girl?'

'Good morning,' Dana's smile glinted. 'I'm fine, thank you, Mr. Rankine.'

'Jeff, please,' he gasped out in horror. 'Well, what do you make of our terror?'

'Which one?' Dana said bluntly, and he burst out laughing.

'Well, there's a few of them around, but the four-legged one I meant.'

'Absolutely super,' she said with enthusiasm. 'He's a superb animal.'

'Yes, he's that,' Jeff agreed thoughtfully. 'I'm inclined to agree with Logan that he won't amount to much, all the same. Of course Brett won't have that. He's got a one-track mind, our Brett. Logan wanted to geld him.'

'Oh no!' Dana said with reluctance.

'It doesn't make that much difference. Not to their track performance. Look at Phar Lapp.'

'I have many times,' Dana smiled, 'at the National Museum. But you're talking about a wonder horse, an immortal. Phar Lapp could have beaten any horse in the world at his top. We're discussing lesser mortals.' She studied her nails for a moment, then announced, 'Dad will come up with a programme for the Prince. A winning programme, I'm sure of it.'

'Do you think so?' Jeff said quite gently.

'Yes,' Dana replied firmly. 'As far as I can remember Mr. Logan believes in a strenuous training programme for his horses. Dad doesn't. Every horse is different, an individual. Dad finds his way round each one of them. It could be the Prince doesn't need hard work to keep him fit.'

'Well, we'll see,' Jeff said absently, and pocketed a pale blue envelope. He looked up casually and smiled. 'I'm taking a run into Melbourne in about thirty minutes. Care to come? I could do with some bright company.'

Dana hesitated on the brink of a polite refusal, then she thought. Why shouldn't I? Father is happy now he's with his beloved horse and dear Margot will be about the house all day. Besides, it would be an opportunity to look at all the marvellous shops, the city arcades that harboured hundreds of boutiques and speciality shops, the endless beautiful parks and gardens.

'Half an hour, then?' Jeff prompted, watching her face.

'Done,' she smiled.

'Good girl! I'll have the car brought round to the front. Wear something really with it—you know, terribly chic. We might have lunch some place you take beautiful girls.'

Dana went out of the room feeling she had let herself in for something. Jeff was a married man. Surely he still didn't see himself as an eligible bachelor? However, she followed his advice and dressed in a rye-coloured two-piece linen suit, with a short straight skirt and a tailored, sleeveless thirties tunic over the top. She did up the gold buttons that marched two by two from the V-neck, down the front to the inset waistband, then tied her hair at the nape with a long silk scarf, tan with white coin spots, and turning the back hair under, looping it in wide folds. Gold earrings, a half a dozen gold bangles, caramel shoes, bag and gloves completed the outfit.

Dana leaned forward to the mirror to give her town make-up a final check, then turned away, satisfied with her appearance. She detoured through the maze of rooms that led to the stairway and caught a glimpse of Brett going into the living room. She heard Margot's clear, rather affected voice, but she didn't hear Brett's reply. Dana decided to chance it and came on down the stairs just as Brett came back into the hallway. He looked up at once and saw her, taking in every detail of her ultra-smart appearance. Dana swallowed nervously, one foot poised above the dull gold-carpeted step. Then she tilted her chin. She didn't have to account to Brett Cantrell for her actions, so why the nervousness? She came on down the stairs, announcing blithely:

'If anyone wants me I'll be in Melbourne for the day.'

One black eyebrow shot up.

'Say that again.'

Dana sighed elaborately. 'I said I'll be in the city for the best part of the day'. She walked over to an antique wall mirror, all scrolled and gilded, and studied her reflection without seeing it at all.

Brett came up behind her, tall and a shade menacing.

'I might be behind the times, but I thought you hadn't a car of your own for the moment. We'll see about that later on if you're so anxious to take off.'

She met his dark eyes in the mirror and dared herself not to look away.

'I'm going in with Jeff. I thought you knew.'

'How the devil should I know?' he said tersely.

'Well, you know everything else,' she retorted sharper than she meant to. Her eyes fell away from his reflected image. It was no use crossing swords with Brett Cantrell. He was a born autocrat.

Brett glanced down at his watch with nervous irritability, then put his hands on her shoulders, swinging her to face him.

'I'm expecting a call from the States any minute. I haven't time to argue with you. Don't go, Dana. There'll be plenty of opportunity for you to run about when I'm ready or your father is. But not Jeff!' He tipped up Dana's chin with one hand. 'Don't go. Do you understand me?'

Margot's voice called a third time, louder and a shade more urgent. 'Brett!'

He swung away from her then and moved swiftly away with long easy strides.

'Do you understand me!' she muttered to herself indignantly, and went straight on out the door. She ran lightly down the steps where Jeff raced the car in.

'All set?' His hazel eyes snapped approval as he leaned forward to open the door for her.

Dana slipped into the bucket seat, smelling of expensive upholstery. 'I hope so.'

He shot her a swift perceptive look. 'Having troubles?'

'No, nothing I can't handle, Jeff.'

He let in the clutch and slid out of the driveway.

'Not many people realise this, but Brett's the image of the old man. Not his old man—Tod. You remember Tod? A law unto himself. Brett's the same. Don't do as I do, do as I say. You know the old "I have spoken".' He sounded deeply resentful.

'Umm,' Dana replied, her eyes closed. Somehow she had no desire to take sides against Brett Cantrell and certainly not against the dead Tod Rankine.

'I don't know how he wangled it, but until he came back from the States the Stud was mine, lock, stock and barrel.'

Dana opened her eyes. 'Tod told you that?'

'Many times.' Dana glanced sharply at Jeff's profile, surprised by the bitterness reflected there. His face seemed thinner, somehow tight and drawn. He went on in a rush. 'What Brett wants, Brett gets—that's his credo. Not that I'm not filled with admiration for his talents. He was a constructional engineer, you know.

Pretty successful too, I gather. Yes, sir, he's clever and he's ruthless. The old man all over again. Using people for their own ends. Tell 'em anything as long as it suits the purpose.'

Dana's voice shook a little, though she tried to control it.

'That doesn't sound like Tod Rankine, or Brett for that matter.'

'Well, it's just a game with them, doll. Way over our heads. But let's relax and enjoy ourselves for a while. Tell me what a girl like you has been doing in that Godforsaken wilderness you were in.'

Unaccountably Dana felt very angry, but she spoke lightly enough.

'You're wrong, Jeff. It was quite beautiful. I love the Outback. I'm just as much at home in the bush as I am in the city. Perhaps more so. Mareeba was a real home to us. I know I'm going to miss it.'

'But men, doll. What did you do for a little scintillating male company?' Jeff persisted.

Dana smiled. 'I must be very dull, Jeff, but I never felt the need of it.' Certainly not your variety, she thought a trifle waspishly.

Jeff snorted. 'Ridiculous doll! You don't expect me to believe it.'

'No,' Dana agreed dryly, and glanced out at the speeding green miles. His next question was more to her liking.

'Do you suppose your father would care to take on a few of my horses?'

'Why don't you ask him?'

'I will, but I thought I'd sound you out first. He used to be the best before the Akura affair. I suppose he's still got his old way with the gees.'

Dana was beginning to wish she hadn't come. Jeff's style irritated her.

'Dad is quite brilliant with horses, Jeff,' she said emphatically. 'He's gentle and considerate. He knows which thoroughbreds need pampering and which ones thrive on hard work. Brett believes in him, and as you implied yourself, Brett never settles for second best.'

'True, doll.' Jeff put his foot down hard.

Dana wound down her window, the cool rush of air reviving her. Jeff was a little too friendly, though perhaps he meant to be kind. She rather liked a little reserve in a man and immediately blinked away the vision of a sombre dark face.

Jeff's hazel, glinting eyes watched her profile appreciatively. 'I can show you a most intriguing little place for lunch. We're both browned off at the moment. What say you do some shopping or what have you, and I'll meet you in the foyer of the Southern Cross about one p.m.? How's that?'

'Agreed,' Dana said slowly, hoping the day would pick up.

'Fine.' Jeff's voice was full of enthusiasm.

The intriguing little place was sufficiently intriguing to make Dana temporarily forget her troubles and the quality of the reception she would undoubtedly get when she arrived home.

Jeff ordered with largesse and considerable aplomb, which was not surprising when you considered he had spent almost half a lifetime at it. People were coming down the narrow stairs moaning with disappointment at the crowded interior. The cellar décor was very cosy, very intimate, with rough-hewn furniture, but the food was superb, the service excellent and the house wines the best.

Jeff attacked his sizzling barbecue steak with relish, piling on the Caesar salad.

'This is the in joint at the moment until the fashions change.'

Dana smiled as she watched the long tanned legs of the girls disappearing back up the steps.

'I can see that, judging by the number of disappointed customers.'

Jeff nodded. 'Try your burgundy. It's very good.'

Dana sipped at it appreciatively. She glanced over at Jeff's down-bent head. His face looked smooth and untouched, a far cry from the bitter young man he had been at the outset of their journey. They ate in silence while Dana looked around the room, quietly enjoying herself. When she looked back her glass had been refilled. The wine and the soft, insistent background music, the cigarette smoke and the subdued lighting were all combining to make her feel pleasantly fuzzy. Jeff's hand, long and surprisingly soft, rested over hers.

'We should make a habit of this.'

'I never make a habit of married men,' Dana said lightly, and withdrew her hand unhurriedly, although she felt perturbed by the intimacy of the gesture.

'I wish you'd break that rule, doll.'

'Please call me Dana, Jeff,' she protested mildly, softening it with a smile. 'I like to feel I retain some individuality.'

'Right, sweet,' he said instantly.

Dana wondered overwhelmingly why she was here, in this little 'in joint', with Jeff Rankine, an unhappy man and unhappily married at that. Why had she come? It was because Brett had told her not to. If it had been her father she had met in the hall, her father who queried the wisdom of her trip, she would have obeyed without question. It was Brett of course who provoked her into what was really a mistake. There were overtones of unhappiness and frustration in Jeff's obvious pleasure in her company. He was an insecure man and potential trouble.

Over coffee, strong and black, Jeff broached the subject of Margot.

'I don't quite know why I ever got married. I'm the perennial gay bachelor.' He stroked his left earlobe. 'No, that's not true, I do know. It was Tod, of course. The little woman, a steadying influence and all that. It was a mistake from the word go. Margot's an odd sort of girl. I can't begin to fathom her. Don't want to either.' Dana was embarrassed and distressed. She didn't want to hear any odd, sad stories.

'Please, Jeff.'

He held up a hand. 'No, listen to me, Dana.' His mouth thinned into a hard pale line. 'I can't keep crushing this down. Something's happened inside of me. I need someone to talk to. You're lovely and you have a compassionate face.' The words so intensely spoken hung in the air unanswered because Dana was stunned by his directness. She knew an urge to run for her life, but Jeff's eyes pleaded with her to be kind to him. He was talking quietly almost to himself.

'I see Brett getting ahead, sweeping everything before him. He's got it made, you know. The lot—even my wife.'

'That's untrue,' Dana thought in despair, and her eyes registered her protest.

'Yes, I know, Margot's making all the running.' Jeff looked at her intently. 'But what man can resist an attractive woman indefinitely? One determined to have him?'

'If there is one, I'm sure it's Brett Cantrell,' Dana said hardily.

'He's got you too, hasn't he?' Jeff's hazel eyes were over-bright, disarming in their directness.

'You're quite wrong,' Dana heard herself insisting. 'But Brett is my father's employer. We're living in his house. It would be extremely indiscreet of me to discuss him behind his back.'

'Yes, I suppose so,' Jeff said tiredly. 'It's hard to take, all the same. Even the house is his.'

For a moment Dana softened towards him.

'Don't dwell on it, Jeff. It does no good. I've a little experience of living with a seeming injustice. Put it out of your mind and go on from there. You're young, good-looking, financially secure, you have a beautiful wife. Why don't you cut loose, make a new life for yourself?'

Jeff was adamant, the proverbial immovable object.

'You don't understand, doll. It's part of me. It should have been mine.' And that was the key, Dana thought tiredly. Jeff would go to any lengths to rationalise his behaviour. She kept hearing her father's voice saying Tod Rankine had made the only possible choice and she stirred uneasily.

In an instant Jeff reverted to his usual gay self, pointing out this or that face in the news. He seemed to know a lot of people and quite a few went out of their way to wave or stop by their table. Dana sat through the introductions, wishing they weren't quite so arch. It would be better for Jeff to take a firm stand with his wife instead of moaning about her attraction to another man. Now if it was Brett! A ghost of a smile touched her mouth at the thought of his reaction to such a situation. If he was nothing else, he was a man—the original dominant male.

Dana was collecting her bag and gloves when a press photographer for the society pages stopped by their table. He was young and slight with very long wavy hair.

'How come you manage to escort all the most beautiful girls, Mr. Rankine?' Jeff flashed his white smile, not displeased by the standard flattery. Dana knew a sharp desire to duck under the table. She was in enough trouble as it was.

'How about a picture, now?' The photographer aimed his flashlight and took a shot before either had time to say, yes or no. Jeff sat back unprotesting, so Dana collected her things saying, coolly:

'Shall we go?'

Holding her head high, she threaded her way through the maze of tables past all the interested eyes. Out in the dazzling sunshine she discovered she now had a headache. Jeff took her elbow to pack her along the sidewalk.

'I've one or two things to fix up. What say I meet you back at the car in an hour?'

Dana agreed, only too pleased to have that much respite before the drive home. Jeff Rankine was heavy going.

She mingled with the lunch-time crowds, crossed the traffic-thronged street and strolling through the arcades on the other side, glad for the moment to be by herself. A cheekily chic boutique run by two clever young designers drew her attention. The casual fashions were too bright and too imaginative to resist. They were great value too, so she settled on two outfits and finally walked out of the shop with three under her arm. A glance at her watch told her she was cutting it fine, so she took a short cut which led to the car park, cutting through a small arcade. The wonderful aroma of freshly roasted coffee beans caused her to turn her head, looking into the dim interior of an expresso bar. Jeff Rankine was sitting at a table for two, his companion a petite ash-blonde. She was very stylishly turned out but quite obviously several years his senior. Neither looked particularly happy, the blonde coldly implacable, Jeff barely hiding his tension and anger. It could have been a lovers' tiff, Dana thought wildly, if they didn't look like mortal enemies. She swerved and ducked her head furtively, hurrying past. It was a good ten minutes before Jeff showed up.

'Sorry to keep you waiting, golden girl. I've been held up at the bank.'

'Some bank!' Dana thought wryly, and slipped into her seat. Jeff Rankine seemed to lead any number of lives. Perhaps the blame for their marital discord didn't lie entirely with his wife. Then thinking of Margot, Dana sighed. Life in the city was getting more complicated by the minute.

CHAPTER SIX

BRETT ignored her little escapade . . . totally; a state of affairs that Dana found even more disconcerting than his outspoken attacks on her. His manner was rather that of a benevolent adult in the presence of a tiresome child, but one that had to be humoured for extraneous reasons. Her father was completely unaware of her jaunt, having spent the best part of the day studying Prince Gauntlett's record, his race efforts, times, track conditions, jockeys, stakes won, when the horse was worked, when spelled, until by the evening he had the facts at his fingertips. As well he made a point of speaking to each member of the staff in turn, from the foreman to the stable boy. It was one of his contentions that much of a trainer's success was due to a loyal and efficient staff.

True to his promise, Brett had given orders that the final decisions as to Prince Gauntlett's training and racing programme were to be left to his new trainer. This pleased Sloan immensely, even if it was the only way in which he could work.

Over dinner the three men discussed horses and bloodlines interminably. Brett had decided to purchase the stoutly-bred New Zealand mare Tamaki, in foal to the up-and-coming stallion Sandown. It was planned to ship her over in time to have her foal at the Stud. The stallion's merits were discussed. Sandown had the reputation for being one of the best performed sprinters in New Zealand.

Margot looked frankly bored by it all. She demanded constant masculine attention and grew restive and irritable if it was not forthcoming. She glanced at the Gregorys with cold hostility. Incredibly the daughter was looking interested in the conversation, the father siding vigorously with Brett's decision to import completely new blood in the form of a notable English stallion whose first crop of runners had had immediate success, but whose blood-lines were relatively unknown to the run of the mill-owner.

Jeff was against it. In his view the stallion was an enormous capital risk. It would not be well patronised, it would not get a full book for the first few all-important seasons, or the top quality mares.

'Surefire success is what we went,' he said forcefully for him, his fair face flushing. 'What about Firebrand?'

'Look, Jeff,' Brett spoke quietly, understating Jeff's vehemence, 'we've reached saturation point there. I've got to follow my own judgment, and I think we can afford to take the risk. We're in the fortunate position to be able to breed slow maturing types—the stayers. The market calls for early comers, I know, but they won't carry off the Cup. Only a top class stayer will last the gruelling two miles. We've got plenty of glamour two-year-olds. This new stallion is a true blue blood. His sire was Star Court, and you're talking about a stayer highly successful in anything from eight furlongs to two miles five furlongs. My mind's made up.'

'In that case, there's nothing more to be said, is there?' Jeff pushed up from the table. His flush had faded, leaving him unnaturally pale. Margot gazed after him almost as if they were bitter antagonists in a secret war. Obviously she was untroubled by thoughts of wifely loyalty. Brett looked unperturbed as usual.

'I think we'll go down and have a look at Summertime's foal—her first.' He glanced across at Dana. 'Care to come?' The dark eyes moved to include Margot.

Margot shivered fastidiously. 'No, thank you, I'll wait here.'

Dana looked pleased and excited. 'May I?'

'You may, though I don't see why treats should be the order of the day,' Brett said repressively.

Sloan Gregory looked from one to the other with caution. He was beginning to suspect that Dana and Brett were incompatible. It sometimes happened that way.

'Well, come along, dear,' he said hastily. 'I must say I'm anxious to have another look at the filly.' He moved to hold Margot's chair, watching her whirl away in a flash of scarlet. She just might have been in a temper! All three decided to ignore it. They went out into the hallway down the steps and into the bright moonlight. A yellow moon swung down the sky and dew lay heavy on the thick springy grass.

Dana walked lightly between the two men, liking the feel of the crisp night air on her face. A flying fox took off with a harsh flap of wings, startling her. She clutched at Brett automatically, murmuring something quite incoherent.

'There's a brave girl,' he patted her arm consolingly, his soft laugh tinged with sarcasm. Dana went to pull away, but he had her now in a firm grasp.

Summertime, a handsome bay with nine straight wins to her credit, lay on her bed of straw with her day-old foal beside her. The mare had been brought in for an expected difficult birth; the filly was lying twisted—but with expert veterinary assistance she had come through the ordeal without damage to herself or her daughter. Summertime opened her eyes and raised her head as Brett flicked on the light. She gazed at the visitors with mild eyes. She had had more than her share of petting and congratulations.

'How are you, sweetheart?' Brett spoke caressingly, his voice gentle with affection. The filly, a chestnut, was soft-eyed with a white blaze and two white fetlocks. All three faces softened automatically as they looked down at mother and daughter.

Dana slipped her hand into her father's. 'Such delicacy and beauty,' she breathed softly.

Her father's hand tightened. 'Yet the same little filly will travel at a fabulous speed over short distances.'

Brett bent down and ran an experienced hand over the filly's legs. The little one did not flinch but lay quietly.

'Nature imposes a penalty, I'm afraid. This little creature doesn't possess the strength or the endurance of your Outback pony or crossbred hack. Man was responsible for the evolution of the thoroughbred, its beauty and its blazing speed potential, and it's up to man to handle it with the right kind of love and patience. In unlimited quantities, as you say, Sloan.'

'Certainly beyond the requirements of most animals,' Sloan agreed quietly.

Dana knelt down beside Brett, her fair head near his shoulder. Her voice was little above an awed whisper.

'There's almost a physical frailty, isn't there? A tangible nervous sensibility.'

The little filly blinked at them with intelligence.

'I've an idea she might be slightly wobbly on those legs, Brett.' Sloan was studying the filly intently.

'Yes, you're probably right. Well, we won't take any

chances. I'll have her clapped into plaster, support the fetlock of each leg. The slight inconvenience shouldn't prove any setback.' Brett leaned over and patted Summertime's neck. 'You've got the makings of a high class filly there, old lady.' Summertime lay back contentedly, waiting for tomorrow when she could race her first-born fetlock-deep across the lush pastures.

Brett turned and looked into Dana's face, so close to his own. Her eyes were long and lustrous, shimmering with emotion very close to the surface. The sight of mother and foal had moved her now, as always. She blinked nervously at him, unable to withstand his expression at once tender and appraising with a depthless insight. He stood up, bringing her up with him. He traced a finger over her short straight nose, soft full mouth, lingered at the cleft in her chin.

'I've just thought of a name for the filly. What would you say to Bright Amber?' His words hung in the air, the implication unmistakable.

Sloan answered for both of them, the pleasure coming into his face.

'I'd say we'd be honoured.' Brett reached up and flicked off the light.

'Well then, let's go back and open a bottle of champagne. If Dana promises to behave we just might let her have some.'

'I'll accept the challenge,' she said in a low swift voice, and was rewarded by the glint of amusement in his eyes.

By morning tempers had risen again. Dana was on her way out for the morning's ride when Brett caught her up in the hall.

'If you have a minute, Dana.' She followed him

through to his study, wondering what was coming. He was wearing his dark sombre look and that had definitely been an order, not a request.

In the study Brett walked over to his desk, opened the morning paper, leafed through it, folded it carefully, then drew her attention to the society pages. Dana glanced down at herself and a smiling Jeff, determined not to show her inner disturbance.

'I didn't think I'd photograph as well as that,' she parried with studied casualness.

'Almost angelic,' Brett agreed grimly, 'but you and I know better.'

She looked up at his tone, biting her lip, but eloquence was in her eyes.

'You're very hard to follow, Brett,' she said slowly. 'Strange and rather cruel.'

'What do you mean?' The challenge was quite clear in his eyes.

'Maybe I'm the one who's strange,' she said, sighing. 'Tell me, why are you angry?'

The full weight of his gaze was on her. 'For some time at least you need someone to tell you what to do, Dana.'

'Yes,' she said, turning her head away and frowning slightly, 'I'm quite sure you can do that.'

'I can and I will,' he bit out forcefully. There was a merciless appraisal in his dark eyes as he turned her back to face him. 'Don't encourage Jeff in any way. Leave well alone. He's unhappy, unsure of himself, above all he's *married*. He's not entitled to your strength or compassion. I won't have you used as a buffer between them. Keep all you have to offer for the right man.'

Dana was trembling. Her head felt hot and feverish.

The angry tears sprang to her eyes.

'I'd better go before I forget you're my father's employer.'

'I didn't mean to hurt you,' he said with rough tenderness.

She whirled out of his grasp, a high colour in her cheeks.

'It doesn't matter a damn who you hurt, Brett! Just as long as you have your way. Just who do you think I am anyway,' she flung at him accusingly, 'Mata Hari?'

'No,' he smiled despite himself, amused at her fiery outburst. 'Lorelei, perhaps.'

She shook her head very slowly. 'You'd be the death of me if I had to put up with you for any length of time!'

He laughed outright. 'Well, you'll have to try until after the Spring Meetings. It's in your father's contract.'

'By the time I count three I'm going to be out of this room,' Dana announced with spirit, 'otherwise I might forget my gentle upbringing.'

'I know how it is,' he said swiftly to her averted face. 'One day you'll be able to talk to me honestly.'

'I'll be too old to bother,' she flashed at him.

He raised his head, his eyes glinting dangerously.

'I'll help you out. One . . . two . . .'

She whirled, perfectly controlled, and made for the door. The handle refused to budge. She closed her eyes as Brett's arm slid past her waist. The lock clicked loudly.

'Allow me,' he said in sardonic undertone. 'I haven't been so entertained in years.'

Dana rushed away from him, the palms of her hands itching.

His voice floated down the corridor. 'Three!'

In the weeks that followed, Dana made every effort to establish some kind of contact with Margot Rankine. It was no use. The older girl made it quite clear that her efforts were unappreciated, and even worse, resented. Not that they saw that much of one another. Margot led a very social life—luncheons, dinners, charity drives, theatre, ballet, concerts with or without her husband as escort. Often she stayed overnight at her parents' town house, or so she said.

Dana was understandably surprised when the older girl knocked on her door one evening. They had had little to say to one another during the day. Margot was going out. She looked tall and very elegant in a sumptuous black brocade glistening with silver thread, the deep V of the neck plunging discreetly. Her thick dark hair was caught back in a Grecian knot and diamonds winked from her small close-set ears. She came to the point at once, her eyes moving restlessly over the furnishings of Dana's room.

'I'll be staying overnight in the city. Brett has some confounded woman coming tomorrow—household help. See to it for me, would you? I can't rearrange my schedule now.'

Dana murmured her agreement. 'Will she be helping Mrs. Mitchell, then?'

'*Replacing* Mrs. Mitchell,' Margot stressed abruptly. 'It seems her only son wants her to join him in New Zealand. He married a New Zealand girl. Damned unsatisfactory, if you ask me.'

'Oh well, then,' Dana said rather vaguely. She couldn't for the life of her think of anything else to say. Margot was decidedly an odd sort of girl.

Margot hesitated for a few seconds longer.

'Turner's her name, a Miss Turner. She's highly

recommended. Think you can handle it?' She sounded decidedly uncertain of it herself.

'Without a doubt,' Dana replied flippantly.

Margot flashed her a look of cold dislike and went back along the hallway. Dana shut her door firmly, then went about preparing for dinner. Tomorrow night it just could be served by the highly esteemed Miss Turner. It shouldn't prove too difficult to interview the lady.

Miss Turner arrived soon after ten the next morning with a youngster in tow. The child, a little girl, was thin and dark and distressingly plain, except for a pair of fine brown eyes. Miss Turner was equally thin without the advantage of good eyes, but she was, according to her references, 'a wonderful asset about the house'. The child presented a problem to Dana and to Miss Turner.

'She's my brother's,' the lady announced in a deafening whisper. 'Poor soul! He and Dot were killed in an auto accident. They were on their way to collect Lally from boarding school.'

'Lally?' Dana echoed faintly.

'Lavinia,' Miss Turner murmured apologetically. 'She was named after me, poor little soul. Now I'm all she's got.'

The child grimaced, causing Dana to look at her more closely. Her gaze was returned by a pair of young—old eyes. Dana knew at once Lally would be hard to manage. She toyed with the blotting paper in front of her.

'I don't think Lally was expected,' she managed at last.

'No,' her aunt agreed unhappily, her brows coming

together with anxiety. A pair of faded brown eyes studied Dana from under the frown. Dana was nothing if not impulsive. The house was a mansion. Surely it could house one small child without inconveniencing anyone?

'Am I going to stay or not?' Lally demanded bluntly.

Dana began to laugh. 'Yes, dear, I think so.'

'You must forgive her,' Miss Turner pushed at her hair, gathering in a few wisps, which immediately escaped again the moment she let go. 'She's been through a lot.'

Dana's soft heart seemed to melt. Poor little scrap. It would be a good life for her here on the Stud. She might even teach the child to ride. It had been one of the great pleasures of her childhood.

Miss Turner studied the young girl opposite her. She was quite beautiful and best of all she had a quality of compassion that didn't always go hand in hand with an abundance of good looks. Hadn't she every reason to know? Lally looked quite different now—calm, serene, more as one would expect an eight-year-old girl to look.

'If you like I'll show you out to your rooms. There's an adjoining one Lally can use. I expect she'd like a nice long drink. A lemonade, perhaps?'

'A ginger ale would be better,' Lally put in firmly. Her voice was more like a little boy's, but the intonation was 'well-brought-up'.

'A ginger ale it is,' Dana said equally firmly.

'She looks almost pretty when she smiles,' her aunt said fondly, and Lally pulled a ferocious face, completely dispelling the momentary illusion.

'Well, she has lovely eyes,' Dana smiled down at the scowling child, but she was now in a mood. 'Do you like horses?' Dana asked briskly.

Lally halted in her tracks and a curious expression crossed her plain little face.

'I absolutely adore them,' she declared passionately.

'Good girl,' Dana said matter-of-factly. 'I'll teach you to ride!'

The child bounded along between them and not for a moment did Dana question the wisdom of her actions.

Margot did. She strode into the living room with her head thrown back, arrogant on her sloping shoulders. Her impatient rush startled Dana who was straightening a magnificent picture of Dame Nellie Melba in her Melbourne Cup finery.

'This is absolutely fantastic,' Margot said, her voice trembling.

Dana met the blue fire gaze head on. 'What is?'

'Don't act stupidly,' Margot said, her temper lashing out of bounds. 'There's a quite dreadful woman on our side verandah and the ugliest child I've seen in many a long day. She tells me she's our new housekeeper, Miss Turner. Is she an unmarried mother into the bargain?'

'Not exactly,' Dana said calmly. 'You're going too far ahead. Young Lally is her niece. Her parents were killed quite recently, the poor little scrap.'

Margot threw down her bag and gloves. 'My God, but you're tiresome!'

'I'm very sorry,' Dana said with unnatural calm, 'but I can't be as *you* want me to be, Mrs. Rankine.'

Margot glanced at her suspiciously. 'Well, you've taken far too much on yourself. What does Brett have to say to all this?'

'I haven't seen the men since breakfast.'

'I thought so,' Margot burst out triumphantly. 'Well,

let me tell you Miss Turner and her niece are out. They can't stay. It's quite ridiculous!'

'It's a very big house,' Dana pointed out quietly, holding on to her temper for Lally's sake. 'It's only one small child, after all.'

'We're not running a boarding house,' Margot replied sharply. Anger put colour under her white matt skin, accentuated the brilliant ice blue of her eyes.

'Perhaps you can make an exception this time,' Dana murmured.

'Your sense of humour is deplorable,' Margot's voice was bristling with rage and frustration. 'Not so surprising,' she added obscurely.

Dana raised her eyebrows trying to figure it out, but Margot turned on her heel without another word and swung out of the room. She was very sure of herself, Dana thought unhappily. Had she reason to be? Had she so much influence with Brett that she could hire and fire at will? She was clearly of that opinion.

Brett wasn't in the house ten minutes before he heard about Dana's quite exceptional high-handedness. From the top of the stairs Dana could hear Margot's high, clear voice rising and falling with the passion of her emotions. Dana hesitated, then decided to enter the fray. She would have to eventually. Brett looked up at once as she appeared at the living room door.

'Come in, Dana,' he said very mildly. 'What *is* this dreadful thing you've done, exactly?'

'I've just been telling you, Brett——' Margot burst out shrilly.

'You're becoming too excited, Margot. Just take it quietly.'

She stared back at him, looking as though she were about to burst into tears.

Dana moved further into the room, very conscious of the accelerated beat of her heart. 'I'm sorry if I've offended. I really thought I was doing the right thing. It's my only excuse, if I need one,' she added a shade louder. 'I can't see how one small child can upset the household. She's a pathetic little creature. I thought I might teach her to ride. The country life will put some colour in her cheeks, flesh on those little chicken bones.'

'It's unthinkable!' Margot looked as if she was about to explode. She lifted her vivid blue eyes to Brett's. 'It's unthinkable, Brett. Please listen to me.'

He looked over her head at Dana.

'Have you anything else to add? Some dresses for the little one, warm clothing for the winter, perhaps.' His face was a bland mask.

'Jodhpurs,' Dana admitted at once. 'She'll be needing those.'

Brett burst out laughing. For a moment it looked as if Margot was about to hurl something heavy, then she turned and flew out of the room.

'She's very angry,' Dana said unhappily.

'With *me*? I thought it was you.'

'Oh, me, of course,' Dana agreed. 'How could I mean to imply you?'

'You've got the nerve to imply anything,' he said quite frankly. 'Just give me time to get used to you, that's all.' He stood up and his gaze was very direct. 'Next time you get the notion to reorganise the household let me know, will you, little one?'

'I'll never offend again,' Dana said with sweet, sincere gravity. She was immensely relieved by Brett's reaction to the situation.

'If I could only put money on it,' Brett said simply.

'All you can do is wish.' Dana kept her head down, her expression demure. He gave a short laugh and walked past her, running a casual hand over her smooth blonde head.

'I'm afraid not, Dana. Our way is pure fight every second.' She turned to look after him questioningly, but he had already disappeared.

CHAPTER SEVEN

LALLY proved an apt pupil. There was no need to instil a feeling of confidence in the child. She took to riding like a duck to water.

'There's only one way to get on your horse, Lally.' Dana was giving her her first lesson. 'Roll on and slip off.'

Lally paid close attention while Dana stood at her mount's shoulder, shortening the reins to a comfortable distance in front of the wither. 'Leave the reins light on the horse's mouth. If you want to turn your mount's head, tighten the near rein by slipping your elbow inside it,' she demonstrated as she spoke. 'Now you've got control of the rein and your pony can turn his head around as you mount. Now watch this closely.'

Lally obeyed, screwing her eyes up in the strong sunlight. There was no need for any reminders. Dana faced the pommel, turned the stirrup and inserted her foot securely, finding the tread of the iron. She seized the pommel with her right hand, dropped her left shoulder back, rolled over the pommel and swung erect as her right leg came down in the stirrup. Lally watched fascinated. With any luck she might do just as well.

Dana then dismounted in the shortest possible time without alarming her horse, slipping over the pommel and pushing herself away, clear of the saddle. Lally followed every move intently, a battered old school hat pulled down over her eyes. With her shirt and shorts and thin wiry legs she looked more like a boy than a girl. She was actually very impressed with Dana. In fact, had she known it, Dana was succeeding where others had failed. Lally was well on the way to bestowing her affections.

The two of them sat on the fence while Dana explained as simply as she could the importance of 'hands'. She would remember until the day she died being told by Bart Prescott, the famous jockey, that she had 'a lovely pair of hands'. The thrill would remain for a lifetime—a natural facility to some, but for most an art that required constant thought and practice. As a young rider her father had put her on a quiet horse and made her ride around an enclosure blindfolded, receiving and transmitting signals along the reins, the give and take, the delicate fingering, the feathery touch of a rein on her horse's neck.

Lally was breathing quickly now, listening to stories of how bushmen, stockmen, flat jockeys, steeplechase jockeys, used different styles and techniques. The lesson proceeded, using a single rein at the bottom bar of a strong curb bit. Lally would quickly learn lightness of hand with this method, Dana had decided in advance.

The next day they came face to face with Margot as she waited for the car to be brought round to the front of the house. Margot glanced at them, preoccupied, smoothing on her gloves, and passed them without greeting, then paused.

'Shouldn't that child be doing her lessons?' she said sharply, flicking a glance at Dana. 'I'm sure you'd make a wonderful teacher.'

'I don't go back to school for another fortnight,' Lally muttered very rudely indeed.

'I beg your pardon?' Margot stared at the child as though she could scarcely credit her hearing. Lally subsided sullenly, almost but not quite intimidated by Margot's look of cold disapproval.

'She needs punishing for that, and she deserves it.'

'Perhaps,' Dana said irritably, annoyed with Lally but just as anxious to defend her. 'Children know when they're being attacked just as much as adults.'

'And the upholder of the rights of children. How sweet and protective!'

'I'm sorry I can't return the compliment,' Dana retorted very smartly.

Lally found the conversation reviving. She looked from one to the other with interest. Dana caught the child's knowing expression and cut the encounter short.

'Don't let us detain you, Mrs. Rankine.'

'As if you could!' Margot's mouth thinned unpleasantly.

Dana and Lally walked on.

'What do you make of her?' Lally asked.

'What was that?' Dana pretended she hadn't heard. Lally repeated the question.

'Well, she's very smart and good-looking,' Dana sidetracked, struck by the almost adult directness of the question.

Lally snorted. 'Some people might think so. But I don't like her.'

'Lally, Lally!' Dana sighed rather helplessly, and proceeded to distract the child's attention. 'I really think you should have your hair cut.'

'Oh, super!' said Lally, fingering her long thin ponytail. 'I've been wanting to for ages. How about like Cilla Black?'

To her credit Dana didn't laugh. 'We'll see,' she said

gently.

The simple suggestion turned into an absolute must. Miss Turner had no real objection, though she 'rather fancied plaits on little girls, but never mind'. Dana decided to go ahead with the idea. She approached Brett that evening after dinner.

'I'd like to speak to you, please, Brett.' A slight nervousness made her sound arrogant. He must have thought so too, for an amused glint leaped into his eyes.

'By all means. Come out on to the verandah.'

Dana followed him, watching him lean negligently against a white column circled with ivy. He waited for her to go on.

'It's about Lally. I'd like to get her hair cut.'

A brief smile touched his mouth. 'Most commendable, but surely you don't want me to cut it?'

'By no means,' she said repressively. 'I wondered if I might have the use of a car. I'll have it done in Melbourne.'

'Good God!' Brett made a sweeping gesture that could have meant anything. 'Do you mean to tell me a small girl needs professional attention?'

'Of course!' In the half light Dana's eyes were like amber velvet. 'She's not really a pretty child, you know.'

'That's a masterly understatement.' Brett almost laughed. Lally's looks had registered with him. Dana ignored this.

'Her hair needs proper shaping. It has a natural wave. It would give her confidence in her appearance. Besides...'

'Yes?' he prompted, the severity of her tone amusing him.

'I thought I might pick out a few outfits for her. Her

current wardrobe is pure Granny Scratch.'

'Indeed?'

Dana moved fretfully. 'Please be serious, Brett. I think it's important—important to a little girl like Lally.'

He moved swiftly and laid a hand on her shoulder. 'If you can delay this momentous occasion until Friday I'll take you in myself.'

Dana gazed up at him, trying to gauge his expression. 'I can only say it's very good of you. I accept your offer and thank you for your generosity,' she said sweetly.

Brett laughed suddenly. 'You're being very extravagant. It's rather becoming for a change.'

She smiled, her mouth parting over her small white teeth. 'I get so few opportunities to impress you.'

'I'm very impressed,' Brett said sardonically, the inflection in his voice disturbing. He looked over Dana's shoulder and saw Jeff watching them curiously.

'So this is where you got to. I've got some film on Brandy Boy's work-outs. Care to see it? Sloan is inside waiting.'

'Yes, I would,' Brett said unhurriedly. 'Coming, Dana?'

They walked back into the light to watch Jeff's most promising sprinter in action.

Lally could not have asked for a nicer day to have her hair cut. It was quite magical, soft and flawless, and the countryside looked as fresh and pretty as a picture postcard. Dana dressed in a short white shift of bouclé-textured jersey and added a black and white Isadora scarf trailing its fringe to the hemline. She snapped on her favourite gold earrings and bracelets, adjusted the strap of her shiny black sandals and added a few more tissues to her roomy black bag, just in case Lally might need them.

Lally was looking a picture, in a grey pleated skirt, mini by accident, a white school blouse, imperfectly ironed, a string of shocking pink beads—Aunt Lavinia's —and a frilly white hat trimmed with pink roses that drew attention to the plain little face beneath it. Dana didn't have the heart to veto any single item of the outfit. Brett did.

'For God's sake get that hat off, child.' He reached over the seat and whisked the offending hat off Lally's unprotesting head. 'It's definitely nanny-goat material.'

The hat went sailing through the window. Lally gazed after it round-eyed.

'Aunty bought that,' she announced solemnly, then burst into fits of laughter.

'The beads too, Dana, there's a good girl.' Brett spoke to the girl at his side.

Lally was already putting the beads in her bag.

'If you don't like them you don't like them,' she said philosophically.

Brett smiled at her, his sudden, transforming smile, 'Atta-girl!'

Lally blushed. At eight, rising nine, she was already conscious of his considerable charm.

Brett turned to Dana with the smile still in his eyes. 'I see what you mean about Lally.'

'You like children?' she said suddenly as though the idea was preposterous.

'Yes. Does that surprise you?'

'A little. You'd like a daughter of your own?' Dana persisted.

His mouth tilted mockingly. 'A wife, then sons, then

daughters, in that order.'

'Goodness!' Dana was much struck. 'You'll have to find a fine strapping woman for that.'

Brett took a bend rather fast. 'Do you think so? A slender wand of a girl would suit me better.' One eyebrow tilted as he took his eyes off the road to glance at her. Dana, like Lally, found herself blushing.

He laughed. 'You've got the wrong idea of me altogether, my pet.'

'Well, it's safer,' she said swiftly without thinking.

A light flickered in the depths of his eyes. 'That's a strange thing to say, Dana.' The inflection in his voice was disturbing.

'Am I to be seen and not heard, then?' Lally asked plaintively, simply dying for attention.

'I don't see why,' Brett answered. 'The very least I can do is ask after your riding lessons.'

Lally obliged, her voice rising with pleasure. She rattled on gaily for quite a quarter of the trip. Now and again Brett glanced sideways at Dana, a smile playing about the corners of his mouth. How had she ever thought it ruthless? A surge of emotion rose in her like new blood. She couldn't put a name to it, she only knew she felt happy.

Raymond was not in the least perturbed by the size of his client. Lally was given the same treatment as a Toorak society matron. She blossomed under all the attention, seizing every opportunity to look at herself in the mirror. The new hair-style, short and feathery with a soft flyaway fringe, lent a certain piquancy to her thin little face. Dana was equally pleased. It gave her great pleasure to bolster the little girl's morale.

Brett met them afterwards and gave a low appreciative whistle.

'Very nice, Lally. Very nice indeed.' His dark gaze lingered on Dana. 'You're a nice child too, upon occasions. Now what would you say to lunch?'

Dana looked apologetic.

'I thought I'd allow Lally to change into a new dress before that, Brett. It would be so much nicer.'

'For whom?' Brett inquired mildly. Enough was enough, he decided with finality.

Lally pulled Dana's hand, unaccustomed colour in her cheeks. 'Navy, Dana, please, with a white collar. I think that's smart, don't you, Mr. Cantrell?' Her shining brown eyes looked straight up at Brett. He passed a hand across his forehead.

'Save us and preserve us!' he murmured soberly. Then his voice changed to its usual incisive tones. 'It could very well be, Lally. Well, come along, girls. I did say I'd take you.' He was rewarded by two pairs of eyes looking at him with sweet, admiring femininity.

'Thank you, Brett,' Dana breathed softly, for once in accord with him.

'Don't thank me, child. Just be quick about it, that's all I ask,' he said with determined good humour, then led them away to the nearest department store.

Lunch was a great success. Lally wore her navy with a thin green stripe and a white collar and sat demurely between Dana and Brett, patting her new hair-style self-consciously. Brett went out of his way to be charming and was succeeding too well, Dana thought with a feeling of alarm.

A couple paused by their table on their way out. She glanced up casually and stiffened. Brett watched her face, his eyes narrowing.

'What is it?'

'Nothing,' Dana said, shaking her head. 'I just thought I knew that woman's face.'

'Magda Ludlow, Ray Ludlow's widow. He was killed in Ceylon. His mount fell on him, don't you remember?'

Dana nodded. Of course, Ray Ludlow. He had been one of the leading jockeys, riding for her father on many occasions. He was, in fact, Prince Akura's jockey that Cup day the champion had failed so badly. Eighteen months and many wins later Ray Ludlow was dead—a tragedy, the papers said.

'You're not telling me the whole truth, are you?' Brett demanded, his voice hardening.

Dana gazed back at him speechlessly. 'Let it go,' he said briefly, and signalled the waiter.

'I don't know what you mean, Brett.'

His gaze brought her up short. 'I think you do,' he said very straightly, and withdrew a few notes from his wallet.

'Are we leaving?' Lally looked happy. 'I do like your car, Mr. Cantrell. It's simply phantasmagorical.'

'Good, Lally!' said Brett, giving the child a second glance. 'In that case Dana might let you sit in the front going home.'

Lally swallowed visibly. 'Oh, may I, please, Dana? It would round off the day.'

'Of course, Lally, of course,' Dana said automatically, avoiding Brett's gaze so intent upon her.

In the car she looked out on the green, speeding miles, her brain working overtime. What would Jeff Rankine have in common with Magda Ludlow? It could be an old affair, but Dana knew instinctively that it was not. Behind the wheel Brett was looking dark and remote. Where had he withdrawn to? And why?

It took a few seconds for Dana to realise that Brett was studying her in the rear vision mirror. She glanced away swiftly. There was some mystery attached to Magda Ludlow, and she meant to find out about it!

CHAPTER EIGHT

AT the end of the month Brett and her father flew to Brisbane for the yearling sales. About five hundred blue-bloods were to go under the hammer. Brett was both buying and selling. The Rankine Stud were presenting a good draft and Brett's colt, Rimmelle, was certain to draw top bids.

For the next few days after the men left it rained. Lally stood looking out on the streaming window, almost but not quite wringing her hands. 'Oh, please let it be fine tomorrow!' Dana felt sorry for her. Each afternoon after school Lally changed swiftly into riding clothes, frantic to get down to her pony. The rain had put a temporary halt to the proceedings.

The days dragged by alarmingly. It seemed quite different without the menfolk, Dana decided with surprise. Yet why that should be so she didn't dare dwell upon. True, Jeff was in and out of the house, but when he wasn't sparring with his wife he was quiet, preoccupied, a man with a problem. Margot was caustic in his presence, withering behind his back. It was obvious, as Lally put it, that 'theirs was not a meeting of true minds'.

Saturday was warm and sunny and the two girls decided to ride out before lunch. Colts and fillies grazed in their separate paddocks, and over against the towering pines mares raced their foals across rising ground. The temperate climate was ideal for breeding racehorses. The mares would be left out in the open and only very occasionally were they brought in for foaling. It was equally rare for weanlings or yearlings to be boxed at night except when they were being prepared for the sales ring. They were left to graze together on the rolling grasslands, fulfilling the herd instinct of the horse, which in its natural state depended on a combination of speed and its own kind for protection. One glance was enough to tell that the quality of the stallions and brood mares was maintained at a very high level. The Stud foundations were based on the horses John Rankine and his son Tod had imported from England, the traditional home of the thoroughbred. The horse was not native to Australia and the old pioneers relied on their imports from the home country. Once settled, the English thoroughbred thrived in its new home.

The two girls rode along in a companionable silence, leaving the property and making a little way into the hills. It was hot now and they decided to have their picnic lunch in the shade of a giant eucalypt at the base of some jutting boulders. The horses were turned out to graze in the sweet-smelling grasses. Aunt Lavinia had taken pains with the lunch. Lally sat with her back against the tree and opened her blue plastic lunch box. An expression of delight crossed her face. Her favourites ... banana and peanut butter sandwiches! Dana knew a moment's anxiety before she opened her own. All was well. Some were ham, others chicken, arranged in a crisp bed of lettuce. She opened the thermos and passed lemonade in a paper cup to Lally.

'I hope there's not a bear up there,' Lally said, pointing back to the rock.

'A bear?' Dana gazed at her in amazement.

'Well, it looks like a bear's den,' Lally insisted, despite overwhelming evidence that there were no bears on the loose in Australia.

There was, however, a large opening between two boulders half hidden by the bushes and vines that swung from the rocks above, that aroused her suspicions.

'Snakes, perhaps,' Dana said conversationally, enjoying her sandwiches.

'Let's go up and see.' Lally polished off her last banana sandwich and raced up the slope.

Dana almost choked. 'Come back, Lally! I'm quite serious about snakes.' But Lally was already at the top, disappearing behind a boulder. Dana put down her lunch and clambered after her. 'This is no time for games. Lally, where are you?'

'I'm here. I'm sliding!'

'You'll finish in Red China if you're not careful!' Dana muttered, and raced around the slippery rocks. Her right foot clutched agonisingly, twisting her ankle as her body swooped forwards. She came down hard. Lally was beside her in an instant, contrition written all over her face.

'Oh, Dana, I am sorry. I wasn't really sliding at all. I'm as agile as a mountain goat.'

'Well, I'm not!' Dana sat up and winced.

'Can you stand up?' Lally asked, her freckles standing out all over her face with fright.

'I hope so,' Dana said with no certainty at all in her voice.

'It's better than getting conked on the head.'

Dana grimaced not only with pain. 'What on earth are you talking about?'

'You could have been hit by a flying rock,' Lally pointed out sensibly. 'Instead you've just...'

'Sprained my ankle,' Dana finished off miserably.

'Hit by a flying rock.'

Dana snorted. 'Hit by a flying saucer, more like it!'

'That's morbid,' Lally said, and leaned forward to have a look at the ankle. 'I think you've just jarred it.'

'Go and put your nurse's uniform on,' Dana said a shade tartly. They met one another's eyes and laughed. Dana examined her ankle gently with cautious fingers. It didn't feel broken or anything. It was swelling rapidly and was very painful to the touch.

'Fractures of the ankle are often difficult to detect,' Lally observed with true clinical detachment. 'When in doubt see your doctor.'

Dana looked up at the incredible child. 'Where do you get your information from, Lally?'

'Textbooks,' Lally said succinctly, and put a frail little arm about Dana's shoulders, heaving ineffectually. 'Try and stand up.'

Dana tried. The sky swooped and then regained its equilibrium. Her ankle throbbed sickeningly. She lifted her face and took a deep breath.

'You'll have to go back to the house, Lally. I don't think I can make it. Get Jeff, like a good girl. I know you can do it.' She felt Lally go rigid beside her. Dana lowered herself to the ground and moved her injured ankle tentatively. 'There's a short cut to the home paddocks over there where those trees are—can you see?'

'I'll get help,' Lally whispered, seeming to grow inches as her voice dwindled.

'Good girl!' Dana repeated matter-of-factly. 'I know I can rely on you.'

'I won't be long,' Lally whispered again. Dana lay back, feeling the pain in her ankle more vividly. She started to pray that Lally would arrive home safely.

Dana opened her eyes. She was lying almost blissfully, warm and content, staring up at the sky and wondering why she was lying there at all.

'All right now,' the voice came from behind her, and she turned her head and looked up. She was lying with her head against Brett, his arms cradling her.

'I think so.' Her voice was dazed and husky. 'I sent Lally for Jeff.'

'I know. I came instead.'

'I've hurt my ankle.'

'I've attended to it until I get a doctor out.'

'Oh,' she said vaguely, unable to look away from him.

Brett lifted her then so that she was held against him more closely, her head resting on his shoulder.

'I'm sorry, Brett,' she said, beginning to tremble. 'I'm a nuisance.'

He held her higher, his grip very firm. 'Yes, you are.' Her long blonde hair had escaped from its ribbon and swung past his cheek.

She felt dreamlike as though she were moving through a phantom landscape her body wrapped in warmth and comfort. The tearing pain in her ankle was forgotten. Even Brett's voice sounded dreamlike to her ears—a voice that could make her respond almost as much as his touch could.

'Dana,' he was saying, 'Dana, I'm going to put you into the car. I'll try not to hurt you.'

Almost against her will Dana put up her hand to touch his mouth and slipped into oblivion.

When she awoke her father was standing by her bed with Lally beside him. The two of them were holding hands.

'How's my girl?'

'Gee, I'm glad you can open your eyes!' The two of them spoke at once.

Dana smiled. 'Hello, Dad, Lally. I see you made it.' She patted Lally's dry little hand.

'In record time too,' Lally said proudly. 'Mr. Cantrell said I'm the right woman for an emergency.' She blushed at the memory.

'And so you are, too,' Sloan agreed stoutly. His blue eyes met his daughter's. 'In any pain?'

'Not at the moment, Dad,' Dana said quite truthfully.

'You will be, dear, as soon as the sedation wears off.'

'I'll read to you,' Lally promised. 'I've got a new book out of the library—*Kim's Wonderful Summer*. You'll love it.'

'Thank you, Lally. I've never had a chance to read that one.'

Lally beamed.

'How did the sales go, Dad?'

Sloan Gregory sat down on the bed, avoiding the patient with care.

'Very well indeed. Rimmelle attracted some spectacular bidding from the Japanese, a very successful session all round. Brett knocked back a six-figure offer for Glengovern. He has double cross blood with Grand Chevalier, you know.'

'If he's as good as I think he is, he's worth a lot more.' Brett was watching them from the doorway. He came in to stand at the foot of the bed. 'Grand Chevalier is probably the most sought-after stallion in the world. His progeny in Australia alone have won over two million dollars.'

'Wowee!' Lally breathed reverently.

Brett smiled and looked at Dana. 'How are you?' His dark eyes were deeply intent upon her.

She lifted her head from the pillow, then lay back again. 'Seeing double,' she said faintly.

'And you think one is enough?'

She twisted her head on the pillow to look at him, colour replacing the pallor beneath her pale gold skin. 'Definitely.' She tried to rally. His voice came to her calm and slightly amused.

'You don't mean that, Dana.' She watched him with fascination, trying to relax herself.

'Thank you for rescuing me, Brett. For the second time, as it happens.'

Sloan smiled at his daughter's sweet submissive tone. He was sure it was only temporary. He stood up, bringing Lally with him.

'We'll take ourselves off, young lady. I, for one, have things to attend to. I'll look in again later on in the evening, dear.' He bent down and smoothed the pale hair away from his daughter's forehead. He straightened, then looked up at Brett. 'I thought I'd give the Prince a work-out with young Boxall up on him. He's got very real ability that lad.'

'This afternoon.' Brett's head shot up.

'Say in about thirty minutes.'

'I'll be there,' Brett said briskly.

'Good—I'll get my things,' Lally added.

'Not you, young lady.' Brett was quite definite.

She looked up at him for a moment with wide eyes, then answered most respectfully, 'Very well, Mr. Cantrell.'

'There'll be plenty of opportunities for you girls to come down later on,' he added, softening the blow.

'I can't wait!' Lally said, going out of the door.

Over her head Sloan winked at them. The room was suddenly quiet and very still. Dana half shut her eyes letting the fading sunlight filter through her lashes.

'I feel quite feather-witted,' she spoke rather rapidly.

'I don't regard that as a serious fault in a woman.'

'I can't believe that.'

Brett smiled faintly. 'Well then, perhaps I should have said I have no objections to your being feather-witted occasionally. In fact I rather like it. It's very instructive.' Her eyes narrowed in puzzlement. There was a pause and he smiled. 'You don't know whether to believe me or not. Your face is the expressive kind, Dana. You can't help showing what you're thinking and feeling.'

'Thank you,' she said, and took a deep breath. 'I'll have to watch myself.' She felt him move to the side of the bed. He seemed very close.

'Open your eyes, then.'

'I can't,' she said very simply.

'This isn't getting us very far.' Brett's voice had a smile in it. Her eyes flew open then, registering alarm. Nervously she slid down in the bed as he sat down beside her. 'You take fright very easily.' He raised his eyebrows and she could see the familiar mockery in his face.

'I do not!' she flashed at him. 'You just have a marvellous trick of putting me at a disadvantage. You make me feel like a complete idiot most of the time.'

He laughed then. 'And you're not?'

She stared back at him, a kind of excitement holding her paralysed. 'You know very well what I'm getting at, Brett.'

'I admit I like to catch you off guard, Dana. Then I see glimpses of a little girl, pale-haired and very pretty in a ruffled dress.'

There was silence between them, the fragile shell, for the tension that flared beneath the surface.

'You're trembling,' he remarked conversationally. It took another second for Dana to realise they were being watched. A flicker of wariness made Brett, too, turn his head. Margot was at the open doorway pale and a shade distraught.

'I heard about your accident,' she said in a dead tone, advancing into the room. 'I thought I'd look in. What exactly is it?'

Brett answered for both of them. 'A bad sprain. It will probably take a fortnight or more to heal.'

'Most unfortunate,' Margot managed indifferently without once looking at the patient. She turned to the door. 'I really must speak to you, Brett, if you could spare a few moments.'

'I think I might, Margot.' He rose, looking down at Dana with an air of detachment. 'It won't be so bad lying there. We'll think of something to keep you amused.'

'That's just what I want to be—amused,' Dana said flippantly.

'Brett!' Margot's voice rose. She sounded very anxious.

Brett turned and walked to the door, sketching a brief salute. As soon as he was outside the door Margot began to speak, the words rushing over one another in a torrent.

Dana closed her eyes again. She felt faintly dizzy. Only now could she admit to herself she didn't feel complete unless Brett was somewhere near her. From now on she couldn't trust herself to glance at him, not a gesture, not a tone would she allow to betray her. She reached out a hand and flicked on the bedside lamp. Her blonde hair and the pallor of her oval face shone with the glow. She looked up at the canopy over her bed with an air of intense concentration.

'I never expected this to happen,' she murmured out loud, then turned her face into the pillow.

A scream brought Dana out of a deeply troubled sleep. She sat up in bed, straining to catch the sound again. Moonlight made the room as bright as day, but the brilliance was not reassuring, for it only deepened the shadows. Was it real or only part of her nightmare? She switched on the bedside lamp and winced with sudden pain. Only a few doors away her father was probably snoring his head off. It was quite true, as he often boasted, that he could sleep in a bus station.

She sat there listening with a rising tension. The house seemed at peace, quietly slumbering. She heard nothing but the faint far-off cry of a night bird. Dana poured herself a glass of water, swallowed another Veganin and lay back.

Her heart was racing. After a while she became angry with herself for panicking and switched off the light with a resolute snap. She punched her pillow into a more comfortable shape, determined to go right back to sleep again. But she lay awake for a long time, watching the changing patterns the moonlight made on the floor. It must have been the bird that she heard and deep in sleep translated it into a scream for help....

Morning proved that it was not. Margot hurried into her room after breakfast, her face white and exhausted-looking.

'It's absolutely wicked!' she burst out as she stood at the foot of the bed.

'I don't understand.' Dana hoped she didn't look as bewildered as she felt.

'Wicked!' Margot repeated almost hysterically.

'I don't think for a moment it isn't,' Dana said soothingly. 'But I didn't do it.'

Margot stood staring at her. 'I know *you* didn't do it. But I blame you nevertheless. I *know* who did it. I've just confronted the ghastly little wretch.' Margot began to pace up and down. 'She's cowering behind the skirts of that idiot aunt of hers. She'll be punished, mark my words. For a child to delight in doing such things!' She gave a gurgling sob. It was obvious she was close to tears.

'What a commotion! I must speak to you.' It was Dana's morning for visitors. Miss Turner stood at the doorway, her expression freezing ludicrously when she caught sight of Margot.

'Commotion? A disgrace, you mean!' Margot almost screeched.

'I must apologise for my niece's behaviour,' Miss Turner began in her most tentative manner.

'I don't *want* an apology!' Margot shouted.

'Naturally you're very angry.' Miss Turner flushed miserably about the neck.

'Angry is not the word. I'm revolted, simply revolted. The child is simply appalling. But what else could be expected?' Margot took time off to fling a withering glance at Dana.

'Are you suggesting it's my fault?' Dana sat up heatedly, not having the foggiest notion what she was getting heated about.

'You're her *friend*, aren't you?' Margot fired at her. 'A fine example! Just what she needs, in fact. Let me tell you, you haven't heard the last of this!' She swept to the door. 'Either of you,' she added vengefully.

Miss Turner hesitated, not knowing what to do, and Dana waved her right into the room.

'What's wrong? Tell me quickly. I can't stand much more of it.'

Surprisingly Miss Turner almost smirked. 'Lally put her guinea-pig in Mrs. Rankine's bed.'

'Good God, that's not really funny, for Margot or the guinea-pig. Besides, I didn't know Lally had a guinea-pig,' Dana sidetracked.

'Oh, she has one all right. Brought it home from school. It's all the rage.'

Dana lay back, feeling quite ill. 'What do you think is going to be the outcome of this?'

'Lally will miss out on a week's riding,' Brett said from the door, surprising both women. 'She has to learn not to play silly schoolgirl pranks, however provoked. Margot was terrified, and so was the wretched guinea-pig. It's no way to treat a pet,' he added sternly.

'I thought I heard a scream.' Dana looked at him suspiciously, but his face was quite bland.

Miss Turner twisted her hands, looking the picture of uncertainty. 'May I go now?'

Brett looked across at her. 'Yes, of course, Miss Turner. I've spoken to Lally and there's no need to punish her any further. She'll be miserable enough deprived of her riding.'

Miss Turner nodded respectfully and left.

'You look pale.' Brett crossed to the side of the bed and opened out the window, then turned back to study the patient.

'I feel pale.' Dana looked briefly at him and away again.

He reached over and ran a finger down the smooth curve of her cheek. 'Why is that?'

'Well, Lally for one thing,' Dana evaded. 'I heard the scream last night, and I thought someone was being murdered.'

'Did it really alarm you?' A smile hovered at the corner of his mouth.

'Petrified me. I'm not very brave, you know, especially when I can't walk.'

'If I'd known that I would have looked in on you, tucked you in with a reassuring peck on the brow.'

'Isn't that rather reckless?' Dana said lightly, but her nerves were jumping about unpredictably.

'Definitely.' Brett looked at her and laughed. She looked through her lashes, determined not to let him think she felt any emotion at being alone with him.

'But you're starting your story backwards, Brett. Why did Lally behave so badly?'

His knuckle brushed the cleft in her chin. 'I'll let Lally tell you that. She was pretty upset, poor little beggar. Margot doesn't pull her punches. Even so, the child's idea of vengeance exceeded even her expectations. That was some scream! No wonder at all you were frightened. And to think I found out too late!'

Dana groaned and shut her eyes. 'Please go, Brett. I can't stand it.'

'Perhaps I'd better, for my own sake.' His voice was very dry, very sardonic. From the tone of it he might have been telling her anything.

Dana didn't have to wait long for Lally's version.

'She told me to take my ugly face some place else, among other things,' Lally said bitterly, sitting on Dana's hand quite without realising it.

Dana retrieved her hand, rubbing it gingerly.

'But why would she do that?'

'She thought it, I suppose,' Lally said without evasion. 'I *am* ugly, so what? But if anyone wants to take a rise out of me they'd better look out. Boy, did she get a fright!'

'Lally, Lally!' Dana was gentle, seeing through the belligerence to the raw hurt beneath. 'Listen to me, dear. What you did was a bit silly—you know that, don't you? A senseless prank, that upset you as much as it did Mrs. Rankine. But most important, you're *not* ugly. Not in the very least. You have fine eyes, for one thing, a great asset to a woman, and a highly individual personality. Beauty *is* only skin-deep, Lally, that's why it's such a famous old saying. It's the woman under the skin that counts—the real woman, with wit and warmth and charm.' Lally looked as if all this did not concern her in the least, so Dana tried harder. 'I'm telling you the truth, Lally. The world's most fascinating women have never been beautiful,' she said with absolute conviction in her voice, not at all sure it was true. Lally raised her head then and looked straight back at Dana. 'So you're never, never, never to think you're ugly again, do you hear me?'

The bitter set left Lally's mouth, but she still looked unhappy.

'It's all right for you, Dana. You're lovely. You don't even have freckles. You couldn't really know about us ugly girls. *She* does, though—that Margot bitch. The only thing I'm sorry about is that I hurt poor old Joe.'

'Joe's your guinea-pig?' Dana said sympathetically.

'Yes.' Lally looked very close to tears. 'He's off colour today. I'd better go to him.' She slipped off the bed and raced out of the room, but not before Dana caught the sparkle of tears.

Damn Margot! Dana thought fiercely. Secure in her

own beauty, to lash out at poor little Lally. Just as she was coming along so nicely too. She lay back in bed, nibbling her bottom lip. What else could she do to improve Lally's appearance? Perhaps her teeth could do with some attention.

CHAPTER NINE

AUTUMN brought in carnival time for Melbourne, the season of 'Moomba'—Moomba had everything. Non-stop sport, spectacles, entertainments to suit every mood, every taste, every pocket.

The carnival racing programme was expected to draw huge crowds to the four beautiful racecourses—Flemington, Caulfield, Moonee Valley and Sandown, all within easy distance of the city centre.

Flemington, the big occasion racecourse, vast in size, and the most beautiful and famous racecourse in Australia since its establishment in 1840, was the venue for Australasia's most famous race, the Melbourne Cup, and the classic events of the Victorian Turf—the Derby, Oaks, St. Leger, and for the principal jumping races, the Grand National Hurdle and the Grand National Steeple. The Moomba programme for Flemington included the Queen's Cup, the Newmarket Handicap and the Australian Cup, over a period of three meetings.

Sloan had entered Prince Gauntlett for the Queen's Cup, a weight-for-age race over ten furlongs, not without some misgivings. He would be up against eight of the best horses in the country, including Jeff's promising three-year-old, Brandy Boy. Brett had the brilliant Cup, on the last day of the carnival meeting.

Dana was almost as nervous as her father over the Prince's chances. Before the Akura inquiry Sloan

Gregory had been supremely confident of his horses, but he had been badly shaken. Still the Prince had been shaping promisingly ever since young Mannie Boxall, the stable apprentice, had noticed the quieten-ing effect the sedate gelding, Sir Kendall, had on his highly strung companion of the paddocks. With the gelding brought to act as a 'tranquilliser', the big black stallion was a normal animal responding to every re-assuring whinny of his stable-mate. The Prince con-tinued to work well although Sloan had not asked him for a serious effort.

Two days before the Queen's Cup, Ken Warwick, leader in the jockeys' premiership, was rushed to hos-pital suffering from an allergy and declared unfit for the meeting. Sloan was left with the decision to call in Garry Hurst, a leading jockey only too anxious to ride the Prince, despite his reputation as a barrier rogue, or back his own judgment and put Mannie Boxall, the sixteen-year-old apprentice, up on him.

As far as Sloan was concerned Mannie was an artist and like all artists born, not made. In Sloan's opinion Mannie was a remarkably good judge of pace, with first-rate hands and an innate love of horses. The same Mannie had cried in the dressing rooms after winning his first race at the age of fifteen—'the happiest day of his life'. Sloan worried the problem over on his own. Brett had left the decision to him after all. Mannie was relatively inexperienced, but he had exceptional natural ability, and most of all he knew the horse. He was, in fact, the only stableboy the Prince would let near him.

Sloan waited until four-thirty a.m., the rising time for stable-boys, on the Saturday morning of the race to tell Mannie. He looked in on the boy.

'You'd better polish up your gear, Mannie. You're riding the Prince today.'

Mannie went pale, but he didn't dither.

'Right, Mr. Gregory. It should be a cakewalk. The big feller's trackwork has been first-class this week.'

Sloan smiled and nodded. 'Well, we'll see how he goes this morning. Bring him round for a trial run in twenty minutes sharp. Mr. Cantrell will be with me.'

'Yes, sir,' Mannie said smartly, and turned away with new life in his step. He was almost trembling with excitement. The Prince had never been worked at his top. Mr. Gregory always maintained that it was pointless to burn up all that speed and power when you wanted it in an actual race. Well, now he had the race and the Prince was a top quality stayer. He was positive he could send him on home.

Dana wasn't all that positive, but she kept it a secret from her father. Not for anything would she say or do anything to upset him. Calm as he appeared to be on the surface, she knew her father was suffering from pre-race tension.

Right up until the Saturday morning of the race Dana debated whether to go along to the meeting. It would be quite a social as well as sporting event. She decided she couldn't. Jeff seemed astonished. Even Margot, superbly elegant in a dress and jacket ensemble of coin-spotted jacquard and a large floppy hat in a matching shade of ice-blue, seemed surprised.

Only Brett and her father understood her curious reluctance. It was a long day for Dana. The house was strangely empty. Lally and her aunt had gone visiting. Once or twice Dana went to switch on the radio for the broadcast race results, but she found she couldn't. It wouldn't make any difference to the final result anyway.

About half past four that afternoon she looked out her window to see the red Monaro Brett was using that day sweep up the drive. The thought struck her like a blow—something had gone wrong! None of the party were expected back until well after six o'clock. Her heart gave a lurch. She realised now how keyed up she had been all day, wondering and worrying about the effect an adverse day would have on her father. Could it be possible he had lost his famous 'touch' along with a lot of his confidence?

She heard the front door open, then raced out along the hallway to the top of the stairs and leaned over the banisters.

'Brett!' She was brought up short by the expression on his face. Brett looked dark and inexpressibly remote. 'Oh, Brett,' she whispered huskily, unable to make the effort to come down to him. Their eyes met, his as inscrutable as ever they could be.

'Oh, Brett!' Dana heard the catch in her own voice.

'No! No! No!' Brett began quietly, the words gathering force. He had looked into her mind and seen her gathering fears and tensions.

'What is it? Oh, please tell me!' Dana flew down the stairs, watching the swift change in his face.

'The Prince ran right out in front and stayed there—three lengths, to be exact. *And* he wasn't even trying.'

She gave a muffled gasp of protest and launched herself at him.

'Why, you did that on purpose, you sadistic...'

He caught her mad rush, encircling her narrow waist and swinging her high off the ground.

'I think congratulations are in order, don't you?' He

set her back on her feet, keeping a steadying hold on her elbow.

'I suppose so.' Dana stood still for a second, trying to match him in sophistication. Then she raised herself on tiptoe and brushed his cheek with her mouth. He drew back with his eyes black and sparkling.

'Is that chaste little peck your idea of a kiss?' he asked smoothly.

'That's my idea of a joke,' she said crisply, transfixed by the look in his eyes, at once serious and taunting.

'Well, the joke's up, little one,' he laughed softly, and turned her chin up to him. His mouth was cool, experimental, deliberately tantalising.

Dana arched away from him, overcame by resentment at her own vulnerability.

'Let me go, Brett. I'm furious,' she muttered against his mouth, and heard his ironic;

'Enchanting! You're always on about something or other.' His arm came round her then with cool precision, gathering her fully into him. The quality of his kiss changed, became deep and demanding. A door swung open for Dana to the dizzying world of the senses, shattering all her preconceived ideas of lovemaking.

She pulled her mouth away before she succumbed completely to his easy mastery. In another minute she would have trapped herself completely, revealing her deepest and most complex feelings for him.

Brett looked down at her, his eyes roaming over her face. She felt it burning feverishly hot.

'I hope that's not what you expect every time the Prince wins,' she said huskily, keeping a tight rein on her voice.

'Well, let's face it, Dana, the kiss is here to stay.'

'Not with me it isn't,' she said tartly.

He laughed, and she turned her profile to him, her lashes beginning to flutter.

'Well, for one I can't promise anything unless you happen to lose your looks,' Brett said with a satirical drawl. 'You're not undesirable, you know, in an adolescent kind of way.'

She swung back to face him, temper flashing from her long amber eyes.

'I'm surprised I can distract you for even an instant. Your tastes lie so obviously in another direction!'

He pulled her to him, his eyes smouldering dangerously.

'Apologise for that!'

'Apologies are beneath me,' she said, wildly unnerved by the glittering look of purpose that hardened his expression.

Lally's voice reached them, shrill and excited.

'Look, Aunty, Mr. Cantrell's back! He's got a Monaro as well, lucky devil!'

'Saved!' Brett bit out through his teeth. 'Somebody likes you.' He released her with a jerk while Dana rubbed her wrists, hearing her own rapid breathing. He couldn't realise how strong he was. She turned away, blinking back the helpless, mortified tears when he said from behind her shoulder:

'Just before you go, little cat, I have some friends coming down this evening—a small celebration party. I want you to give the performance of your life, if only for your father's sake. Try and act as if you like me. Do you understand?'

She whirled on him then, almost hissing the words at him.

'Mr. Cantrell, they'll most probably go away thinking I'm madly in love with you!'

To her surprise and annoyance he swung away from her, laughing.

Brett's idea of a few friends turned out to be thirty people or more. Dana hesitated on the threshold of the crowded living room, deciding she didn't know any of them. The French windows were all opened out on to the terrace, and the breeze blew the filmy curtains in and out like pale frosted flags. Everyone in the room looked smart, elegant, the sophisticated partygoers. The bar was in full swing and rounds of cocktails were floating from the living room out on to the terrace. Dana's eyes came to rest on Brett of their own accord. His dark head was bent to a rather luscious-looking redhead in a short spangled shift the colour of polished chestnuts. He seemed absorbed in her animated conversation, his dark eyes attentive and amused.

How foolish to imagine he would be aware of me with a roomful of good-looking women, Dana thought wryly, and walked over to where Jeff was standing quite alone, staring down at his drink.

'How goes it, Jeff?'

He looked up at once a smile coming into his eyes.

'Dana doll,' he said clearly, 'you're the best-looking woman in the room.' His hazel eyes had the hard, clear look of the expert. 'A blonde in black lace is still the sexiest thing there is, believe me. Your hair is terrific too. You should part it in the middle more often. Those little side curls! Terrific, doll!' He let his hand rise and fall as though he had run out of adequate words to express his admiration. There was a great deal of chatter and laughter coming from the opposite end of the room. Brett was telling a story, and the faces around him, especially the women's, wore an air of utter absorption. Dana caught sight of Margot, her pale skin flushed with excitement, and was struck afresh by the effect Brett had on her.

Margot looked almost vivid, a statue come to life, in blue chiffon highlighted with diamanté and gold braid at the high neckline and sculptured waistband.

'You'd scarcely credit it, would you?' Jeff was looking at Dana with a twisted smile on his lips. She sensed in an instant that he had read her thoughts accurately, for his expression hardened. 'Now you see what I mean about Brett Cantrell.'

Dana felt uneasy and a little guilty. 'I think you're exaggerating the danger, Jeff.'

He smiled at her almost pityingly. 'Do you?'

Beneath his lassitude, the air of being the perennial playboy Dana was uncomfortably aware of the desperation there. Her face softened momentarily.

'You're becoming too introspective, Jeff. You're making yourself unhappy for no good reason.'

He laid his hand over hers.

'Don't doubt me, Dana. I like to feel someone is on my side. Now let's stop being so dramatic. Come with me and I'll find us a drink.' At the other side of the room Brett looked up in time to see them pass out on to the terrace. A frown gathered between his brows.

It was cool outside. They lingered, making light desultory conversation. The stars had appeared in a cloudless black sky and a brilliant white moon tinted the house and garden with silver. The sharp scents of the night were something to savour, but the warm glow from the house and the thought of another drink beckoned Jeff inside again.

Dana was relieved to see him go. Jeff's unhappiness

had a way of wearing off on her. He was crippled with envy for Brett—and envy was still one of the seven deadly sins.

Couples drifted in and out from the living room to the terrace moving with familiarity about the beautiful house.

'My, my, they let all sorts of people into these parties, don't they? Hello, Karen, Paul.' Dana heard Margot's high clear voice and looked round for cover. She needn't have bothered, for Margot was determined to speak to her. Dana looked up as Margot came towards her, but she didn't say hello. Margot studied the other girl for a moment, disliking what she saw. Good-looking herself, she saw no reason why another woman should be even more so.

'And where's my dear husband?' she asked, her lip curling.

'Getting himself another drink, I imagine. He's rather fond of it,' Dana said shortly.

'Are you telling me?' Margot raised her black, arching brows. 'Well, don't get any ideas that he's fond of you too. Even if blonde *is* his colour these days, or so I'm told, Goldilocks.' Margot's eyes narrowed unpleasantly.

'Isn't that nice?' Dana said carefully, startled by the innuendo.

'Don't waste time on him, my dear. I don't want him, but I know someone who does, extraordinary as it may seem. Jeff's all façade with a great big hole at the centre.' She laughed a small tinkly laugh without any mirth or pleasure in it.

'I wouldn't know about that, Mrs. Rankine, but I do know you're wrong about another woman,' Dana found herself saying. 'It's not what you've been led to believe at all.'

Margot looked at her long and hard and neither spoke for a minute.

'What kind of a game are you playing?' she demanded, visibly losing colour.

'I'm not playing any game,' Dana said cautiously. 'Somehow I'm getting caught up in a situation I've no wish to be in. I saw Jeff with the blonde woman you must be talking about, and believe me, there's no romantic attachment there.'

'And would you know?' Margot said darkly.

'I think so.'

Margot hesitated. 'And why should I believe you?' she asked, her face rigid.

'I don't care if you do or you don't. In any case, as you're constantly telling us, you don't give a damn about Jeff either. Or do you?' She twisted her head to look up at Margot.

'If I did it was a long time ago, believe me. Before I met a real man.'

Dana groaned at Margot's look of utter longing.

'Would you excuse me, Mrs. Rankine, I think I see my father. I've really no head at all for intrigue.'

'Well, stay out of them, that's a warning,' Margot said viciously.

Dana moved away from her swiftly, not looking back.

Inside the house were gay voices and the sound of dance music from the stereogram. Over at the bar Jeff was leaning against the counter staring into the bottom of the glass. It was almost ten o'clock and supper was being served. Dana was caught up by two very consciously sophisticated young men who proceeded to try and outdo one another in monopolising her attention. Supper was sumptuous, as the guests were quick to appreciate. Dana glanced down the crowded buffet tables where her father was standing looking relaxed and happy in easy conversation with a stylish matron in her fifties. He looked up, caught Dana's eyes and winked. She smiled back at him.

Through the open doors she could see a solid black sky studded with stars and the story-book moon. Strangely enough she wasn't in the least hungry. Her two companions were, and argumentative into the bargain.

'Go away any place,' David was saying to Chris. 'Just go!'

Dana felt enormously older and wiser than either of them. She smiled at one and then the other, and order was soon restored. They were back to their elaborate byplay which just missed being absurd, Dana decided a little wearily. To an onlooker she presented the portrait of a poised, self-sufficient, very beautiful young woman, who was also faintly bored.

'Excuse me,' a voice said at David's elbow.

'Hi!' David swung round to smile at Brett.

'May I borrow this aloof young woman for a moment?'

'Aloof?' they queried in unison.

'If that's aloof I'm all for it in women,' Chris grinned back at his host.

'You obviously said the wrong thing.' Dana narrowed her eyes at Brett as his hand closed on the soft flesh of her upper arm.

'Mmm,' he sounded unconvinced. 'Precisely at this point we'll leave, Miss Gregory. See you later, Dave, Chris.'

The two young men smiled and turned back to the table to argue the point out.

Brett held her arm firmly as they threaded their way through the room, out on to the terrace, and down into the garden. It was white with moonlight, the shadows a deep purplish black. Dana quickened her pace, fighting off Brett's restraining hand. In her haste she stumbled against the side of the rock garden and gave a gasp of near pain. That was her weakened ankle. She still favoured it. Brett gathered her back on to the path.

'What are you trying to do, commit suicide?'

She gave an absurd little laugh.

'I might be persuaded to if you're going to read me another lecture.'

'And why would I want to do that, you charming child? Aren't you everything a young woman should be—modest, virtuous as a choirgirl, clever with your needle?' Dana laughed, a soft sweetly feminine laugh bubbling with amusement. His dark eyes found her glimmering profile. 'That's a very pretty sound, little one. I don't hear enough of it. But then you never really relax with me, do you?'

Her eyelashes fluttered. 'It would be more than my life's worth,' she said obscurely.

'What on earth are you talking about?' Brett looked at her with mock curiosity.

'I don't know,' Dana said truthfully. 'It just occurred to me. I never do when you're around. And there's your answer, I suppose. You throw me into a perpetual dither. In fact I'm constantly telling myself you do it on purpose.'

Brett wedged his arm imperiously under her own.

'I'm not looking for trouble, my child, least of all from you. But now that you've started on the subject may I just say one thing?'

'Please do,' she sighed audibly. 'You will anyway.'

He laughed and kept walking across the lawn away from the house. Dana looked back once. The laughter and the music mingled with the sounds of the garden at night. There was a momentary hush as Brett turned her to face him.

'You can guess what it is, Jeff . . .'

'Oh . . . I see.' Dana's eyes moved out over the velvety darkness. She was conscious of wanting to avoid Brett's eyes. He held the point of her chin.

'It must have occurred to you that Jeff is trying to enlist your sympathies, play upon your compassion. You're too young for the job and too inexperienced. You could never handle it properly. I'm concerned that you'll only become involved in a rather distasteful situation. Margot is working herself into a dangerous state of mind. It would take very little to set her off.'

'Yes, I suppose so,' Dana answered wearily. 'What is it you want me to do, Brett? Ignore Jeff completely?'

He felt the agitation beginning to rise in her. 'Now don't fly off at a tangent,' he said gently. 'Just steer clear of him. It's difficult, I know, but then I imagine life is never easy for beautiful women until they find the right man to look after them.'

Unaccountably Dana fired at once. 'What a pity Margot missed out on the right man,' she said sharply, driven by an irresistible force.

He held her face firmly between his hands, shaking her warningly.

'I thought perhaps you'd come at that again. But haven't you picked the wrong place for it?'

Turbulent emotions began to wash over her. The night seemed to close in on them, throbbing with tension. 'Haven't you picked the wrong night for it?' she managed at last. 'There's a couple coming towards us now,' she invented wildly.

Brett turned his head and in that brief instant Dana broke swiftly away from him.

Under the camphor laurel a long trailing branch caught at her hair and secured itself in the golden coil of her nape. She put up her hand in a frenzy of impatience, feeling her hair pull out of its confining pins.

'Oh, damn, damn, damn!' she swore softly.

'More haste, less speed.' Brett released her with cool efficiency. 'You don't seem to have much luck, do you, my pet?' he drawled sardonically. 'Wouldn't it be easier to just give up?'

'Oh, goodness!' Dana tried to ignore him, conscious now of her altered appearance. 'I must look frightful!'

There was a slight pause while Brett studied her with interest.

'No, I wouldn't say that, little one. Rather deliciously dishevelled, perhaps.'

She gave a forced, light laugh. 'Really, Brett, you're quite intolerable, aren't you?'

He met her coolness head on. 'Just as I thought, we might be friends.'

She brushed at her hair ineffectually. 'My requirements for friendship are quite exacting, Mr. Cantrell.'

He laughed softly. 'Do you think I'll ever qualify?' he asked in a slightly bantering tone.

'Is it absolutely necessary you should?'

Brett reached up a finger and ran it over a leaf.

'Frost,' he observed smoothly. 'In more ways than one. But never mind. Intriguing as it is here, I really think we should go back to the house.' He glanced down at her as she tried to rearrange her hair to its former polished perfection.

'Use the service lift to get up to your room. No one

need ever know you've been fleeing through the night from a dark stranger.' The laughter in his voice was apparent.

'I hope not,' she answered repressively. 'It wouldn't do to arouse any more suspicions. Two dire warnings are quite enough for one evening.'

Brett glanced at her sharply, but said nothing. They walked back in silence across the soft springy grass.

When Dana reached the hallway she saw the door of her room standing open, and the lights blazing. She stopped short in consternation. There was not the slightest doubt she had forgotten to turn the lights off. It was a well ingrained, conscientious habit of hers. She hurried along the corridor and stopped on the threshold. Margot was standing facing the open window, her back rigid, an unfailing barometer of her true feelings.

She swung round to face Dana, her eyes glittering strangely. It was a far-fetched idea, but at that moment Dana had the frightening feeling that Margot was dangerous. Characteristically she launched into speech.

'Is there something I can do for you, Mrs. Rankine?'

Margot seemed unable to look away from the shining disorder of Dana's hair. She stepped forwards a little and involuntarily Dana stepped back with the dismal thought that Margot was about to strike her.

'So *this* is your game!' Margot hissed, in a soft deadly undertone. She can't possibly hurt me, Dana told herself severely and crossed to the dressing table.

'I'm afraid I'm not with you, Mrs. Rankine.'

A breeze blew the door shut, startling Dana still further. In the mirror she could see Margot's eyes fixed on her unwaveringly. Dana couldn't stand it. She couldn't wait there tamely for Margot to lash out at her. She swung back to the older girl.

'Well, what is it, Mrs. Rankine? I'm going downstairs in one minute.'

Margot seemed transfixed. At last she spoke slowly almost painfully.

'How does it feel to have Brett make love to you, his arms around you, his mouth on yours?'

'I beg your pardon?' Dana parried coldly.

'Answer me!' Margot advanced on her furiously, her voice choking with anger, and Dana recoiled instantly.

'If it were any of your business, Mrs. Rankine, which it is not, I still couldn't answer you. The state of my hair which seems to be causing you so much unwarranted torment was caused by nothing more than an overhanging camphor laurel branch. Please set your mind at rest. Your worst fears are unfounded.'

Margot released her ragged, pent-up breath.

'You just could be telling the truth,' she said finally, her hand dragging on the fine material of her gown. Dana turned away to the mirror and swiftly repaired the offending hair-style. Her hands were shaking, but she ignored them. She fixed her attention on her face, making a pretence of freshening her make-up. Thank God her lipstick was fresh and impeccable, otherwise Margot would have flown for her throat.

She glimpsed the other girl's profile and a shiver ran along her spine. Margot Rankine was definitely disturbed on the brink of who knows what? Dana turned round.

'Are you coming, Mrs. Rankine?' For answer Margot crumbled, completely and utterly.

'No, I'm not!' she shouted wildly, her creamy skin showing a pronounced pallor.

'Are you ill? Can I get you something?' Dana looked down at her thick dark hair, completely nonplussed.

'You can get out!' Margot's voice rose alarmingly. But Dana had had enough.

'Aren't you forgetting this is *my* room?' Margot ignored her, weeping unrestrainedly. She crumpled up over the armchair, the picture of desolation.

'I think I have it in my heart to feel sorry for you,' Dana said slowly, almost to herself. There was a brisk tap on the door, then it opened. Dana looked back. Brett stood just behind her, his face a grim mask.

'What in God's name is going on here? You might remember before you indulge in girlish squabbles that there are guests in the house!'

'Bully for them,' Dana said ungraciously. Girlish squabbles! Margot was a cornered tigress.

Margot lifted her tear-stained face. It was a pitiable sight and it definitely did not suit her, Dana decided dispassionately.

'Brett, oh, Brett!' Margot's voice was charged with emotion, husky and tormented. 'Please take me away, back to my room. I can't stand any more of this.' She shuddered all over her slender frame. 'That dreadful girl ...' she gestured towards Dana, who pulled what she hoped was a dreadful face. Brett seemed to sigh, but his voice was gentle, soothing, almost as if he were talking to a child.

'Come along then, my dear. I'll tell the others you've a sudden migraine. You've been living on your nerves too long.'

He assisted her to her feet, keeping a protective arm around her. Margot subsided against him gratefully, and to Dana's eyes longingly.

'Maybe now I can have my room to myself,' she said

tartly, stung by the sight, in spite of herself.

Brett gave her a hard, speaking glance.

'Be downstairs in two minutes. People just love to talk.'

She flew ahead of him and opened the door. 'It's so nice being here with your family,' she said sweetly, then trembled at the glittering look of reprisal that flashed from his eyes.

Dana said nothing of her troubles to her father. He was a new man among his beloved horses, on the go from four-thirty in the morning, the same rising time as his staff, until after sundown.

The answer to her own problem of course was a job. She waited until after dinner to approach her father. He took the idea in his stride, seemed to be expecting it in fact.

'What are you thinking of doing, dear?' He sounded as if she only had to decide on something to fill all the requirements.

Dana laughed. 'Heavens, Dad, I'm nearly twenty-two, but it's a sorry fact I've never done a day's work in my life. There's very little I can do.'

Her father protested. 'My darling girl, you were indispensable at Mareeba. If you don't call that work, what do you call it?' he asked in astonishment.

'Cutting out cattle won't be of much advantage in the city, Dad. I think the only thing I could do perhaps is model, if any of the agencies would take me.' There was a worried intensity in her voice, and her father almost laughed. For all her exceptional good looks his Dana was strangely without vanity.

'I don't think you'll have the slightest trouble, dear. A little bit of training, department and whatnot, and you'll be well on your way.'

'I hope so, Dad,' Dana said earnestly.

'There's nothing worrying you, is there?' He shot her a searching glance.

'No, Dad. I don't hit it off with Margot—you know that. But the main thing is I've too much time on my hands, especially with Lally at school.'

Her father smiled.

'See what Brett has to say,' he said surprisingly, and Dana's delicate black brows shot up.

'Brett? What's he got to do with it? If it was up to Brett he'd come up with a dozen good reasons why it wouldn't work out.'

'What wouldn't work out? I'm not intruding, I hope.'

Brett strolled out on to the verandah with a crystal tumbler in each hand. He passed one to Sloan, who smiled at him, then sat down beside Dana.

'Well, my child, I'm waiting. A dozen good reasons, I think you said.'

Sloan sipped his drink of whisky and water. 'Dana is thinking of modelling for a living. She feels she has too much time on her hands.'

'Modelling?' Brett turned a professional scrutiny on her and against her will Dana felt her colour rising.

'I can't think of one,' he said at last.

She looked at him suspiciously. 'You think I could do it?'

Brett glanced across at her father and smiled. 'Let me congratulate you, Sloan. Such modesty is very refreshing.'

Dana quietly simmered. The sardonic note in his voice always riled her. He looked over at her down-bent head, the bright overhead light turning it into a glory.

'What are you doing now?' he asked, not trusting her seemingly demure silence.

'Counting to ten,' she said mildly.

Brett laughed. 'You certainly have a calm way of getting angry!'

'Don't let it fool you.' She sparkled a look at him, then turned to her father. 'I think I'll go up to town first thing in the morning.'

CHAPTER TEN

PRINCE GAUNTLETT was sent north for the winter, stabled at Brisbane's leading establishment. It was a common practice for southern owners and trainers to send their horses up for the Queensland racing carnival and to enjoy that State's superb winter climate. By the time the Spring Carnival was ready to get underway in the southern States the horses were returned healthy and rested, ready to be worked towards the peak of condition.

The Cup was already beginning to dominate the conversation in racing circles. Every brilliant stayer in Australia and New Zealand was undergoing solid preparation for the two-mile Melbourne Cup—Australia's High Carnival. Racing circles simmered with speculation. Prince Gauntlett's remarkably improved performances, coinciding with Sloan Gregory's return to the Turf, had not gone unnoticed. Conflicting reports were received that the big stallion was still hard to handle and Sloan Gregory was exhibiting all his old magic with racehorses. No one quite knew what to believe. The Prince had won the Brisbane Cup by eight lengths and in record time, proving beyond doubt that he was a magnificent performer, but it was a known fact that he always travelled in the company of his stablemate and his own personal attendant, the rising young apprentice Mannie Boxall. After his Brisbane run the stallion was turned out for the winter. Sloan Gregory was very individual in his methods. Even so it was quite clear that Brett Cantrell and his new trainer fully intended to carry off the Cup that year.

Dana found she had little time to miss her father while he was away. The career she had embarked upon so tentatively had taken an enormous upward swing. She was now in demand for parades and photographic sessions, and her beautiful face, its bone structure even more prominent by a weight loss, was becoming familiar to the subscribers of glossy fashion magazines. One afternoon a week she acted as house model for Cecile Magnin, the reigning queen of Melbourne's haute couture. It was difficult for Dana to forget her first meeting with Madame Magnin.

She had been sent along by her agency as a possible replacement for Verna Matthews, a top model, an impossibly slender blonde, who had announced her intention of furthering her career overseas; Madame Magnin was known to have a decided preference for blondes. Dana approached the fashion house with some trepidation. It was austerely elegant, its colour scheme the neutral colours of nature, from almost white into sand, into brown, with a fitted carpet of charcoal. Against this neutral background the Magnin creations shimmered like dreams. It was a master stroke of decorating not immediately apparent to the eye.

Madame was small, very dark, much too plump, her hair carelessly caught in a knot, wearing a grey jersey dress under a matching jacket. She looked anything but a brilliant designer, with a passion for creating wonderful clothes. She just might have passed as the clever little dressmaker down the street. Her skin was pale, very matt, her mouth dedicated, but her eyes, once she began to speak, flashed with a kind of controlled ardour, an intensity, a complete single-mindedness, that had earned her her enviable reputation.

She looked Dana up and down, this way and that, at once calm and excited, then in a bell-toned contralto began to point out what she thought was wrong with her prospective model. Once started Madame became voluble, and Dana listened in some bewilderment. Over the short period she had been modelling she had become accustomed to the occasional lavish compliment from the professional circle, praise not easily won. Madame's valuation came as a shock. Dana was reminded almost irresistibly of the pain Lally must have felt at being called ugly. Madame tore her 'walk' to shreds, dwelling heavily on 'raw material'. Just as Dana decided to terminate the interview of her own accord Madame announced ecstatically, 'But the skin texture, the tonings, the eyes and the hair—it almost inspires a collection!' She began to talk of evening dresses, harmoniously elegant, her own master creations and thus incredibly perfect. Her eyes were lit with a vaguely religious zeal. In the end she told Dana to report the following week.

Lally, for one, was delighted. She now felt free to delve into Dana's ever-growing make-up kit, the additional hair-pieces, the expensive accessories that were necessary to her profession. Dana caught her at it one evening calmly trying a short blonde stretch wig over her own dark hair.

'It's true, it's all true!' she piped in a high sweet falsetto. 'You too can be beautiful.' She started to giggle helplessly, then swivelled round to show Dana the full effect. The blonde hair clashed with her olive skin tones, but the style was strangely attractive.

'You look irresistible,' Dana said smilingly, putting

her head on one side to observe the effect. 'I'm quite sure you'll grow up to meet an intriguing young man called Norman who'll have incredibly green eyes.'

'Most probably glass,' Lally finished off very promptly. 'It *is* adorable, though, isn't it?' she caressed her synthetic mop. 'Could I possibly take it to school one day? It makes me look like one of the beautiful people.'

'Not to school, Lally,' Dana said firmly. 'But I just may let you wear it all Sunday afternoon.'

Lally beamed extravagantly. 'You're as good as you're beautiful, Dana. I even said that to Mr. Cantrell and *he* said "You're too damned beautiful." Can you beat that? I'd hug that to myself for a lifetime.' She wound her arms around her own slender little person and rocked backwards and forwards on her heels. Dana listened to her little friend ramble on with only half her attention. It was quite true; Brett acted impossibly remote and condescending these days. Occasionally he openly disapproved of her small coterie of escorts. Even her loss of weight under Madame's instructions had called forth the caustic comment that they would soon have to shake the sheets to find her, and Lally's eyes widened.

'I don't believe you've heard a word I've said!' she said accusingly.

Dana paused and laughed. 'Of course I have, dear. Melissa Marshall is an awful liar...'

Lally found this reassuring.

'Yes, and what's more...'

Dana drifted back to her own thoughts. She wasn't really that thin, was she?

Half past seven found her dressed and waiting for

her date that evening. She was being taken to a new play starring her favourite, Googie Withers. She felt happy and mildly excited and conscious of doing justice to one of Madame's creations. It was purely on loan, an advertisement for the Salon. Dana ran a hand over the sheer layer of metallic glazed black crêpe, sleeveless and V-necked, flaring into pleats with a matching coat of black and gold striped evening dazzle.

Brett came into the hallway just as she was going down the stairs. She felt his eyes on her with heart-stopping impact. She stood still quivering under that brilliant dark gaze. She didn't want to move. She didn't even want to go forward. His voice was abrupt.

'That neckline is a bit extreme, isn't it?'

The colour came up under her skin. 'I don't think so, Brett,' she said coolly. She didn't add that she had gone to the trouble of pinning the plunging V unobtrusively. 'You know, you sound exactly like a fusty old uncle.'

'Really?' he said softly, the inflection in his voice unutterably disturbing. 'Why don't you come down, then?'

She obeyed at once, her head held high. She was being silly, she decided firmly.

His hand shot out and encircled her wrist as she went to pass him. 'Fusty old uncle, I think you said?'

She broke away from him in a panic, her heart lurching. 'I think I heard Reggie,' she said breathlessly.

Brett gave a short laugh. 'What sort of name is *that*?' His eyes were black and glittery.

Dana looked away from him hurriedly, flying out into the stars.

'Tell *Reggie* we expect you home before midnight!'

Brett's voice reached them, heavy with sarcasm, just as Reggie was holding the door carefully for her.

It was quite hot in the dressing room, almost oppressive. Dana was very thankful the afternoon was nearly over. Chrissie, the little fitter, who looked exactly like a squirrel, zipped her into Amber Frost and threw its long matching paisley scarf around her throat with tremendous aplomb. The two women exchanged a smile and Dana hurried back to the showroom. Behind the silver drapes she hesitated and composed herself. As soon as she set foot on the thickly piled carpet she got the now familiar sense of a festive occasion.

Perhaps thirty or forty of Madame's exclusive clientele were seated on spindly white and gilt chairs along with a fair assortment of husbands and what-have-you. Madame sat alone in the midst of all this, the natural centre of her universe. She was, to a marked degree, the only woman present who wasn't well dressed, but she *was* exactly herself—no airs, no graces, no sophisticated woman playing at working for a living. To her clients she was simply Cecile, but Cecile with a difference. She was a direct creative impulse.

Immediately Dana made her entrance, Madame launched into an exhaustive description of the gown and its 'object'. Everything was revealed save the price. Amber Frost was received with great enthusiasm and fingers itched towards cheque-books tucked comfortably into expensive handbags. Dana pivoted and glided back towards the curtained entrance. Her last number was the highlight of the showing—'Spring Rhapsody'. It had been designed with her in mind, pinned on her; an extravagant creation, a full-length evening gown in white floating chiffon, strewn all over with hand-made roses centred with crystals and brilliants, works of art in their own right.

The gasps of admiration were sincere and spontaneous. Dana showed the gown beautifully, identifying with it completely. She moved with undeniable authority and grace, inherent qualities but fully developed under Cecile Magnin's faultless tutelage. Dana's smooth, effortless glide was almost halted by the sight of Margot Rankine's pale patrician face craned forward in a mixture of annoyance and admiration. She was seated towards the back of the salon, a mink jacket slung carelessly over the back of her chair. Standing directly behind her, leaning against a slim fluted column, was Brett, looking smooth and assured, perfectly at ease among a predominantly female gathering. His eyes met Dana's, dark and direct, a sardonic smile lurking in their depths.

Her training stood her in good stead. She passed twice up and down the centre of the room, so that each client had ample opportunity to have a good look at the gown, then disappeared through the curtained entrance. By the time she got back to the dressing room Dana had almost forgotten to breathe. Thank God it was the end of the day!

Chrissie helped her out of the gown, flicked at the skirt with a forefinger and placed it lovingly over her arm.

'Good girl!' she patted Dana's arm encouragingly. 'You know, I'll be sorry to see this one go. It's exactly you. But never mind, dear, some wicked old scarecrow will try to squeeze into it. Isn't that the way of it?'

Dana laughed and slipped into her white silk robe. Chrissie went out and a few minutes later there was a tap on the door.

'Come in,' Dana answered automatically, leaning down towards the mirror. All that eye-shadow would have to come off! Brett stood just inside the door, returning her startled gaze without speaking.

'Yes, Brett?' She tried to be casual—too casual, for his expression sharpened.

'I understand you're finished for the day. I'll take you back with me.'

Her face clouded. 'No, thank you, Brett,' she said decidedly.

'I'm quite alone.' He sounded testy.

'Oh, in that case I'll come,' she smiled, suddenly enchanting.

He regarded her with interest. 'Now what kind of eyes would you call those?'

She smiled. 'Blatantly beautiful, I hope,' she said lightly, and proceeded to remove eye-liner and successive sheer glazes of colour. It was Dana's turn to be curious.

'Am I to hear your valuable opinion?'

'You do very well, Dana.' He raised one black eyebrow expressively.

'The gowns, I meant,' she said sharply.

'Oh, the gowns,' he repeated dryly. 'The last one was superb. If I hadn't known it was you, I would have thought it some impossible dream,' he added with gentle sarcasm.

Dana shook back her heavy fall of hair. 'You're a fearful tease, Brett!' Her eyes went dreamy. 'Yes, it is an impossible dream, in more ways than one. Chrissie, the little dresser, said it will probably be sold to some wicked old scarecrow.'

'What a sacrilege that would be,' Brett said lightly. 'It's so obviously you, my angel.'

She clicked her tongue impatiently. 'I must ask you to wait outside, Brett. You're a disruptive element. I won't be two minutes.'

'I shall begin counting,' he said gently, and shut the door firmly after him.

Margot was furious. She came into Dana's room looking round as though she half expected to see changes. Dana watched her uncertainly.

'What is it, Mrs. Rankine? I'm very busy this morning.'

'Dear me, yes,' Margot spat the words out, 'we are busy lately. I'm very lucky to have caught you.'

'You'll catch me leaving, if you don't come to the point,' Dana answered aggressively, her amber eyes gleaming.

Margot blinked. 'Very well, then. It's about Spring Rhapsody.'

Dana swung round. 'Yes! You want it. Want me to get it for you.'

Margot went rigid. It was rather like watching the sea whip up into a storm. For a few seconds Dana thought the fury in those icy blue eyes would spend itself in physical violence, and she stepped back instinctively.

'I want that dress,' Margot struggled to get control of herself, 'and I'm going to have it. Magnin tells me it was created especially for *you* and that it's been withdrawn from the collection. I don't follow that at all. She was just fobbing me off. And she'll pay for it! My custom must mean quite a lot to her.' She fired a glance at Dana. 'What do you have to do with this? A mere clothes peg!'

Dana's thoughts were jerked back to the present. For

three years Margot had reigned supreme at the house. She bitterly resented another woman's intrusion even if that woman represented no possible threat to her position.

She sighed and picked up her hairbrush.

'I know nothing about what happens to the clothes I model. Cecile does not discuss any aspect of her business with me. I merely model for her. Very occasionally she may ask me what I like or dislike about a particular model. That's it, I'm afraid. Obviously with such a beautiful gown as Spring Rhapsody she was bound to be inundated with orders. Perhaps it was her way out of a dilemma.'

'Rubbish!' Margot said violently, her face sullen with scorn.

'Well, I'm afraid I can't come up with anything better,' Dana said stiffly. She walked to the door and pointedly held it.

'Your rudeness and indifference is quite what I expected.' Margot's voice sounded as controlled as though she could hardly bear to speak. Her great eyes glittered in her pale face. How easy it was to anger and disturb her, Dana thought wearily.

'You know perfectly well you're being unreasonable, Mrs. Rankine,' she said, trying to be patient. 'I'll sound out Cecile if it will make you any happier.'

'Do that,' Margot said in a low voice. 'I badly want that particular gown. Brett found it quite beautiful.'

Dana almost slammed the door, then rested against it thankfully. After a minute she began to laugh, a full-throated laugh with the merest suspicion of hysteria in it. It brought a measure of relief.

'I don't appreciate your questioning me like this,

Dana. I never discuss my business, as you well know.'

Dana turned around slowly so that she was directly facing the table.

'I'm sorry, Madame. Mrs. Rankine was so upset I thought I'd risk it.' She sounded very apologetic.

Cecile Magnin permitted herself the luxury of a snort.

'Upset? That one? She's like her mother.' Her plump hand fell back and forth. 'The egocentricity of them! Spoilt by wealth. They simply do not appreciate their own capriciousness. My monsters, I call them. Still, where would I be without their bank balances? Enough to say the gown has been spoken for.' She glanced up at Dana appraisingly. 'You know, my dear child, every designer dreams of creating for elegant, beautiful women, but that doesn't necessarily mean they *sell* to them. Suffice to say, in this case I am entirely happy. Now go along, child, I simply can't spare you another second.'

Dana murmured her thanks and left hurriedly, and Madame returned to her drawing board. She was smiling.

Outside in the busy street Dana thought tiredly: 'Well, I've tried. Not that Margot will appreciate it.'

CHAPTER ELEVEN

DANA opened her eyes, smothering her first instinct to go right back to sleep again. It was her birthday. She flung up from the bed and went to the window, shivering a little as the tingling morning air attacked her bare skin. I'm at the beginning of another year, she thought, and looked down at the roses climbing beneath her window. Their delicate pink heads were moving in the breeze. High in the sky a silver dart of a bird began to warble in ecstasy. 'Twenty-two,' she said out loud. 'Just think of it!' She turned and walked to the mirror, regarding herself speculatively. She felt quite different, enormously adult, a woman, yet there was at least one person who thought her little more than a child.

'Are you up?' Lally's voice demanded outside her door, high and firm.

'Just a moment!' Dana slipped into her robe and went to the door. Lally was there, and her aunt. Both of them looked flushed and intense and each held a parcel.

Dana smiled. 'You've remembered my birthday!'

Miss Turner thrust a green cellophane parcel, tied with purple ribbon, into her hands.

'Happy birthday, my dear. I could never thank you enough for your kindness to Lally, to both of us,' she said fiercely, and turned away as if in mortal anguish. Dana felt deeply moved. She called after the fleeing figure:

'Thank you so much, Miss Turner.'

'She had to go,' Lally hissed confidentially. 'She's no good at this sort of thing.' The child thrust out her parcel. 'Happy birthday, Dana,' she said gruffly, then immediately ducked her head and pummelled into Dana, bursting into tears.

Dana moved back into the room and sat on the bed, still holding her small friend.

'Now that will do, Lally. You're not allowed to cry on my birthday,' she said firmly. 'What's this, I wonder?'

Lally drew back immediately, trembling with eagerness.

Dana opened her parcel with a great show of interest, catching a small bottle of Apple Blossom perfume as it dived to the floor. She set it down gently on the bed and turned up a fat sketchbook. There were sketches of everybody; several of Dana. Dana turned one vivid page after the other. The colours were brilliant, even violent like the child herself, but the drawings were extraordinarily well formed, easily identifiable. It was quite obvious that there was a wealth of talent there, waiting to be tapped.

'Well!' Lally demanded fiercely.

'What on earth does your teacher say?' Dana countered.

'She wouldn't know,' Lally said scornfully.

'Well, I think you're very good indeed, Lally. You must have proper training.' Dana studied several sketches of horses, Prince Gauntlett among them, then turned to the last page, where she stopped abruptly. She knew that face. Lally's amazing natural ability had caught Magda Ludlow's implacable expression, stark and comfortless. Speaking carefully, Dana asked:

'Where did you see this lady, Lally?' She pointed to the sketch and looked directly at the child.

'That's a friend of Mr. Rankine's. She was down here a few weeks ago, the day Mr. Cantrell had my watch fixed.'

Dana's mind flew back. That would have been the day of the Spring showing. She felt unreasonably upset by Lally's admission.

'What was she doing here, do you know?' Dana was troubled by the need to question the child.

'Oh, she wasn't here long, just sat in the car for about twenty minutes waiting for Mr. Rankine. I watched her from upstairs. Her face sort of interested me—smooth on top and nasty underneath.' She clapped a hand to her mouth. 'I'm sorry, Dana, do you know her?'

'I've seen her about,' Dana said ruefully, then changed the subject. 'I'm delighted with these, Lally. I'll treasure them. I'm quite sure in the years to come they will be worth money. And I've always longed to have some Apple Blossom of my own. Now I really think we'll have to arrange proper art lessons for you. In lots of ways these drawings are much better than I could ever manage.'

'Why, have you had lessons?' Lally's eagerness bubbled into her voice.

'Four years at secondary school. I know the rudiments and I have a certain facility, but nothing like your potential, I assure you. Here, find me a pencil and we'll do a better job of Prince Gauntlett. I'm not too bad at horses.'

'Just wait a second, I'll get one.' Lally flew off the bed. 'I'm no good at animals.' She raced out the door, almost knocking Sloan Gregory down.

'What's happening here?' Sloan's blue eyes lit up with amusement. 'Happy birthday, darling.' He bent and kissed his daughter's smooth blonde head. 'Right hand pocket,' he told her. 'For my little girl.'

Dana smiled and drew a tiny package out of his pocket.

'Big girl, Dad. I'm twenty-two, remember.' She unwrapped the package and snapped the lock of the small box. 'Break it to me gently, Dad. It's gold, isn't it?'

'Gold-coloured,' her father smiled.

'Gold,' she insisted softly, and held up a pair of lacy gold earrings set with yellow sapphires and pearls. She clipped them on immediately and gathered her hair behind her ears to show off her finely chiselled features. 'Thank you, Dad. They're absolutely beautiful.' She smiled at her father. 'But if anyone else gives me a present, I'm going to burst into tears.'

Lally ran in, a beaming little figure. 'Try this for size.' She thrust a drawing pencil at Dana.

Sloan Gregory was looking through the sketchbook. 'Good gracious!' he exclaimed in delight.

'They're mine,' Lally said proudly. 'At least they're Dana's now. For her birthday. She said they're going to be worth money later on.' She smiled widely as Sloan began to pump her hand.

'Congratulations, my dear. What a talented young lady you are, to be sure.'

'Have you seen the sketches of Dana? I think I've made her incredibly beautiful.'

Sloan looked down at a sketch of his daughter in black and yellow and scarlet. Amazingly, despite obvious technical deficiencies it *was* Dana. He turned the pages slowly and like his daughter came up short at the last page.

'The face is familiar, but I can't quite place her.'

'Just a friend of the Rankines',' Dana said quickly.

Sloan shot a glance at her and smiled. 'I didn't know they *had* a mutual friend.' The curiosity died out of his face.

Dana bent her head, absorbed, while line by line she brought a thoroughbred stallion to life. It was a very good drawing. Lally stood stockstill beside her, motionless with concentration.

'There,' Dana said. 'You can do it on your own now.'

'Not as easily as that,' Lally ventured.

'You will, Lally. You will. I can promise you that.'

Sloan went to look out the window. 'By the way, dear,' he announced casually, 'I've got young Reggie to organise a bit of a party for you. Just the usual young crowd. Brett was most obliging about it. He'll have one or two people himself. Round off a bit of business with pleasure.'

If he wanted to create a mild sensation he succeeded. Dana paled.

'A party, Dad, and Brett's in favour of it?' She stopped hastily. Her father was beginning to look unsure of himself. 'That will be marvellous,' she finished off gaily. 'What's it to be, formal or informal?'

'Formal,' he smiled, his confidence in the idea returning. 'I thought you might enjoy it more. Girls always seem to like dressing up, Brett tells me.'

Does he indeed? Dana thought wildly.

'Can I come?' Lally asked hopefully.

'Not tonight, dear. We'll have a party of our own at tea,' Sloan said mildly. 'You'll be a young lady soon enough.'

Dana gazed unseeingly at her father. She had the

uncanny feeling that the party might not go off as planned.

It was mid-morning before she saw Brett returning from the training runs. She just happened to meet him on the gravel approach to the stables.

'Good morning, Brett,' she said demurely.

He smiled. 'Happy birthday, little one.'

She feigned surprise. 'I didn't know you were up on such things, Mr. Cantrell.'

'You disappoint me, Dana,' he said dryly. 'But come along—I do happen to have a little something set aside for my favourite sparring partner.' He was relaxed, completely at ease as he paced her back to the house.

'Tell me,' she begged, glancing up at his dark profile.

'Sorry, it's a surprise.'

Dana shook her head. 'I can't begin to follow you, Brett.'

'Quite right, too,' he said with easy mockery, and led the way through the house to his study. Dana kept her eye off the box labelled 'Cecile Magnin' with great difficulty. Brett touched her cheek lightly, almost a caress, and she trembled.

'There's no mistake,' he said dryly.

'I must be incredibly slow-witted. I still keep thinking there is,' she said slowly.

Brett glanced at her briefly. 'Well, open it.'

Dana hesitated just a fraction of a second, then she went to the table and snapped the wax that tied the label. She knew what it was before she opened the lid.

'Oh no, Brett!' she whispered, between reverence and dismay. All the same she lifted it out and held the filmy white chiffon against her, her eyes reflecting its extravagant beauty. 'Oh no, Brett,' she repeated dazedly, 'I can't possibly accept it.'

He smiled. 'You haven't the excuse that it won't fit.'

'But it's so *personal*!' She flushed under his gaze. 'And it's too darned expensive!'

He tilted her chin up. 'Value is hard to assess, little one. I'm not of the opinion that you and this particular dress should be parted. It seemed so from the beginning and I see no reason to alter things.'

She darted a glance at him from under her long beautiful lashes, then looked away again.

'Oh, please don't tempt me, Brett. I can feel myself weakening, and I must be strong.'

'What for?' he said lazily. 'I like weak women. Well, do you want it or not? I'm sure there's some old dowager dying to get into it.'

She flushed. 'Oh yes, please, Brett. It's the most beautiful dress I've ever owned.'

His dark eyes flashed mockery. 'I'm sure it's only the first in a long line of beautiful possessions.'

'Now don't spoil it, Brett.'

'No,' he said slowly, and smiled. She reached up then and brushed the side of his mouth with her own.

'Thank you, Brett. I can't begin to fathom you, but thank you for a wonderful present.'

He cupped her face in his hands.

'Very occasionally I see the glimmerings of quite a woman,' he remarked lazily, 'then it's gone in a flash.'

She smiled at the familiar sardonic note in his voice.

'It's no use, Brett,' she said sweetly. 'I refuse to fight with you today.'

'No sparks?' he said, his eyes narrowing.

'No sparks!' she stressed gently. It was a promise she fully intended to keep.

By eight-thirty everyone had arrived. The house was aglow with lights and flowers, the bright, beautiful flash of party dresses. The sounds of pop music and young laughter, easier by the minute, came from the living room and the terrace.

Dana drifted in with her dancing partner, almost breathless from her exertions. She was only twenty-two, but she felt positively ancient when faced with Reg Lindsay's enormous verve. She accepted his offer to go and find cool drinks with something like relief. She looked around the room slowly, trying to collect her scattered wits. Within the space of five minutes Reggie had told her he was 'quite mad for her—desperate to marry her—and fully expected to have enough money saved by the end of the year to see England and Europe in style.'

Her eyes flickered towards Brett almost compulsively. It was quite frightening, the physical reactions he aroused in her. And in Gina Cory, if she was any judge! The tall, willowy brunette, a fellow model, had her silky black head tipped enticingly to her host, her pose blatantly female. For the first time in her life Dana experienced a great wash of jealousy. Gina Cory was a fascinating dish—even she could see that!

Reggie came back with champagne and Dana allowed him to take hold of her slender golden arm and lead her away. No one could deny that it was a good party. The large room pulsed with chatter and laughter, the violent innuendoes and gossip. Swirls and eddies of people formed and reformed here and there and couples drifted backwards and forwards to the terrace for dancing. The cheek-to-cheek style had replaced earlier gyrations.

Gina Cory took the first opportunity to draw Dana

into a corner.

'My God, what a dangerously exciting man!' she marvelled. 'And you *live* here with him!'

'Under the same roof,' Dana amended crisply. 'As you can see, it covers a fairly sizeable area.'

Gina ignored her. 'I could go crazy for him, honestly I could. And he's not *married*!' She gripped Dana's forearm. 'Tell me, where is he now?'

Dana vehemently denied any knowledge of Brett's whereabouts.

'You're out of your mind,' Gina said pityingly, and pretended to saunter off in quest of her host.

Just before supper Dana noticed Jeff slip through the front door. Both he and Margot had been otherwise engaged for the evening. She went out into the hallway after him.

'Jeff?'

He put his hand over the banister, managing a faint grin.

'Hello, birthday girl. You look a vision.'

'Are you coming down again?'

'Thanks for wanting me, sweet, but no. I'm absolutely whacked.'

Dana gave him a searching look. He looked more than 'whacked'. He looked gaunt, almost ill. On an impulse she followed him up the stairs. He seemed surprised, but waited for her calmly. Dana approached him directly.

'What's wrong, Jeff? You look quite ill. Isn't there something one of us could do to help you?'

He gave a tired grin. 'You're imagining things, sweet. Just burning the candle at both ends.'

'No, Jeff,' she said quietly, and he shrugged.

'All right, then, I'm in a mess of my own making. But nothing I can't get out of.'

Dana threw caution to the winds. 'Is it Magda Ludlow, Jeff?'

He reeled away from her, almost as if she had struck him. His face was suddenly bleak.

'How in God's name did you know that?'

'It *is* Magda Ludlow,' she said, wanting to probe deeper without rousing his anger.

'Oh yes,' he said quietly, then his voice grew stronger. 'But you know how it is, Dana. You start a harmless little affair and before you know where you are you have a possessive woman hanging around your neck.' He tried for a grin. 'Never become possessive, Dana. It's a woman's downfall.'

Dana felt suddenly cold. Jeff was trying to supply her with a plausible story, but she knew with certainty that he was lying.

'You ... knew her before your marriage?'

'Yes,' he said ruefully. 'Before *and* after, and I haven't the faintest idea how to get rid of her. God knows what she sees in me, but there you are.'

Dana looked away at last. She had to. There was something so false in Jeff's story. She put her awareness of it down to intuition, a powerful and often infallible force in a woman's reckoning.

'I'd like to help you, Jeff,' she said carefully. 'I don't like to see anyone making themselves ill and unhappy, but first you would have to want to help yourself.'

Jeff swung away from her without another word. It was obvious that she had pierced his façade.

'Give me three guesses what you're doing up there!' Brett's voice floated up to her, sounding faintly hard, and Dana walked to the balcony.

'I was just asking Jeff whether he was going to join us,' she said warily.

'And?'

'He's not feeling well,' she answered lamely, and her heart gave a queer lurch. Brett looked hard and dark and watchful. She felt as if she was hurtling without warning from light into darkness. Brett paused significantly.

'Well, you've done your good deed. Come on down. Everyone's waiting.'

Dana knew better than to argue. She came down the stairs and slid her arm through Brett's, walking back to the party.

Margot was there, quite relaxed, even complacent, until she saw Dana. The evening turned freezingly cold. Dana had the shivery feeling that Margot was about to create a scene. She looked deadly, her eyes drinking in Dana's beauty, her wonderful gown, as if they were poison.

Momentarily Dana wavered, but Brett's hand imprisoned her like a caged bird.

'May I present the birthday girl?' he said with easy charm, and the moment of chilling panic passed. Everyone began to clap and to chatter. About one thing Dana was right—Margot was livid.

The rest of the evening seemed to pass in a dream. Dana was steeped in a trance, so much so that she failed to take account of Reggie's unprecedented burst of passion on the deserted terrace.

'I don't wish for many things,' Reggie said quite untruthfully, and reached for her hand, 'but I do wish you'd fall in love with me, Dana.' He knew for certain that she was a million light years away.

Brett coughed dryly.

'Don't let me interrupt you, my children, but would you mind shifting your car, Reg? You're blocking the drive.'

The young man looked mortified. 'Yes, indeed,' and he came away from the balcony and hurried back through the house.

Dana turned her head away to the garden, a little afraid of the false sense of bravado that was growing in her.

'What a charming scene,' Brett said lightly. 'That boy's in love with you.'

She did not deny it, but said coolly, 'Don't make it sound as if he's to be pitied!'

'Did I really sound like that?' His tone was deceptively mild.

Immediately sensitive to his mood, Dana swirled away from him and sought the shelter of the great flowering tubs of camellias at the far end of the terrace. She broke off one flawless bloom in a panic as she felt Brett coming after her.

'I wonder why you're so wary of me,' he said softly. 'Your eyes and your mouth, even the way you turn your head—they give you away completely.'

Dana unfurled the petals of the camellia with shaky fingers. 'Say it,' she said quietly, throwing the flower away.

'Say what?' he said lazily. 'That you're not unlike that camellia? No wonder at all poor Reggie lost his head.'

'You're being deliberately insulting, Brett,' she said huskily, disliking the laugh in his voice.

'How's that, you ridiculous child?'

As always with Brett she felt the blood pounding in

her temples and a sudden strange anger within her.

'But I don't have to listen to it,' she said swiftly. 'I'm going inside.'

'Are you?' he said a shade grimly. 'You make me feel cheated, Dana. I'm quite sure I'm entitled to something better than that.'

'If you are, I don't see it,' she said coldly, perturbed by his look of lean, dark violence.

He did not speak, but reached out for her with a deliberation that made the voice die in her throat. He had never kissed her quite like that before—hard and hungrily and quite plainly possessive. She felt a rising tide of passion within her and pushed away frantically.

'Stop it, Brett, or so help me I'll scream!'

'Scream,' he said brutally, and covered her mouth with his own, effectively stopping all her struggles. She felt the helpless tears beat behind her eyes. She just couldn't bear it!

Brett released her abruptly and she looked up at him almost in alarm.

'Why do you do it?' she demanded in a voice that trembled.

His mouth was hard. 'Because I like kissing you, Dana, the only thing about you I *do* like.'

She felt suddenly degraded and swung up her hand in a positive fury, her eyes blazing amber fire. He caught her wrist in mid-air and held it fast.

'Temper, temper!' he said in a deadly undertone. She managed to pull away from him in an effort to regain control of herself.

'You're about the worst kind of male, Brett. Do you know that—brutal, born to dominate women?'

'And you won't be dominated?'

'Not by you, Brett Cantrell. I can't even see why you

waste time on me when there's . . .'

The expression that flared into his eyes was truly frightening. Too late she took stock of his height and strength.

'Please, Brett,' she stammered. 'I'm sorry. I didn't mean it.' The tears came into her eyes in earnest as she tried to twist away from him.

'Such a transformation!' he taunted her. 'From a spitting wildcat to a helpless little kitten with great drowning eyes! Well, it won't wash, my lady, let me tell you.' In the shadows he was darkly, arrogantly intent on her.

Dana stood her ground, amazed that she could do so.

'Oh, Dana! Brett!' Within seconds they assumed an expression of complete normality, as Sloan Gregory came towards them, smilingly happy.

'Oh, there you are. Some of our guests are leaving. We'd better see them off properly.'

'Of course,' Dana agreed. 'Brett and I were almost at the point of arguing. We seem to clash over just about everything,' she said lightly.

Sloan brushed his hand across his high forehead. 'Everything?' he said unbelievingly. 'You know something—I despair of ever seeing you two friends.' He smiled over at Brett, then linked his arm through Dana's. 'I'm only hoping you'll both come to your senses.'

Dana padded aimlessly round her bedroom, unable to cope with the idea of undressing. She walked to the dressing table and unclipped her earrings. That was a start. What a night! What a totally disturbing, unsettling night! There was a knock on the door and she turned, feeling a prickly sensation under her skin. Margot Rankine thrust open the door without any further ado.

'Oh, my God!' Dana murmured aloud. She was in no condition to do battle with a neurotic, lovesick woman. 'It might be an idea if I put swing doors on my room,' she said, giving the idea her full consideration. 'It would make things so much easier.'

Margot shot her a darting look of venom.

'If there's one person I despise in this world it's a liar, and that's what you are!'

Dana appeared quite calm, although she could feel her head whirling. She looked hard at the other girl, and the thought crossed her mind that Margot was a trifle unbalanced. She spoke her thoughts aloud.

'You need help, Mrs. Rankine, professional advice, and pretty soon.'

Margot burst in on top of her, not even hearing her.

'What other explanation can you possibly give?'

'For *what*?' Dana said fiercely, beginning to lose her own temper.

'For the dress, you fool. The dress that should have been mine!'

Dana wavered. The dress! She had almost forgotten the dress.

'It was a birthday present,' she said mildly. 'It *is* my birthday, would you believe it.'

Margot looked at her in utter disbelief, then she gave an unpleasant sneer.

'The Gregory fortunes must be improving. Perhaps your father . . .?'

'From *Brett*,' Dana interrupted steadily. She braced herself for what was coming, knowing she was treading on very dangerous ground.

'So!' Margot's tone no longer shocked her, but the expression in her eyes did. There was murder there. Margot's control lasted only a few seconds, then she sprang at the other girl, crying out incoherently. Dana put her hands up instinctively to protect her face, and felt the sheer bodice of her gown give way under Margot's tearing, grasping hands. With an almighty effort she brought up her own hand and hit Margot as hard as she could across the side of the face. Margot reeled, her patrician face unrecognisable, her pale creamy skin suffused with colour.

'Margot, are you there?' a voice cried out frantically from the other side of the door.

Dana moved swiftly over to it, feeling considerably shaken. Jeff was outside looking white and haggard, with Brett hard behind him. Suddenly all panic vanished, leaving her in icy control.

'What's wrong?' Brett asked bluntly, then swore violently as she moved away from the door. The chiffon of her bodice was rent from neck to the waist, revealing the tiny strapless underbodice.

'Swing doors,' she repeated bitterly. 'There's absolutely no privacy whatsoever.'

'Are you hurt?' Brett bit out, not sparing a glance for the huddled figure on the bed. Margot was as white as death, moaning.

'No,' Dana said crisply. 'A few scraps and a bruise and a ruined evening gown. Nothing to signify, I assure you.'

Jeff went to his wife and was repulsed for his trouble. Brett turned on him.

'For God's sake, Jeff, get your wife out of here. Take her anywhere. Just get her out!'

'You fool,' Margot sobbed bitterly. 'You mistaken

fool!'

'Now,' Brett said, and there was so much command in the single word that Jeff obliged instantly.

The two of them were alone in the room.

'What a wonderful evening,' Dana said emotionally. 'What a perfectly wonderful hell of an evening!'

Brett glanced at her sharply. 'I really am sorry.'

'You're sorry!' she plunged in. 'She's demented—you know that, don't you? Off her head, and about *you*. You must have encouraged her, that's the only explanation.'

Brett swung round with an oath. 'So help me God, I've had about as much as I can take this evening!'

Dana's voice shot up half hysterically. '*You've* had all you can take! Isn't that just like a man? *I'm* the one who was attacked.'

'And I've just done a couple of hundred dollars cold, among other things,' Brett struck the palm of his hand with his clenched fist. 'Don't goad me into doing something I'll forever regret.'

Dana shook her head, breathing hard. There was a sound behind them and they both spun round to see Sloan Gregory standing in the open doorway, a black silk dressing gown over his pyjamas. His expression defied description.

'What in heaven's name is happening here?' he demanded, staring hard at Dana, then Brett.

'Nothing serious, Dad,' Dana said unsteadily, miserably aware of her tattered appearance. 'Margot Rankine just attacked me, that's all.' Her voice broke and she began to shake uncontrollably. In the next second she was gathered up into her father's comforting arms.

CHAPTER TWELVE

DANA woke at eight. It took a few minutes to remember that it was Sunday. Her more immediate concern was that she had a headache and her stomach felt distinctly uneasy. She would have given a great deal to turn over and go to sleep again, but she had promised to take Lally out on a sketching expedition.

Eventually she hauled herself out of bed and began to put her things out. The headache and the uneasy feeling in her stomach persisted so strongly that she began to wonder whether this was merely a result of last night's scene or if she was coming down with something.

There was a sudden tap on her door and Margot burst in without waiting for an answer. She was fully dressed in a superbly tailored suit, a vibrating fusion of pinks and cyclamen. Dana closed her eyes against the fierce wave of nausea that was threatening to swamp her. In another minute she would show how sick she was.

Jeff came to her assistance in hard pursuit of his wife. 'Come away, Margot. Haven't you done enough?' He grasped her roughly by the shoulder.

She shook him off angrily. 'Drop dead!' Her eyes flashed back to Dana. 'So it's true!' she exclaimed fiercely.

Dana opened her eyes wearily. 'My God, not another riddle!'

'Are you coming?' Jeff tightened his grip on his wife.

He looked white and strained as though it were all too much for him.

'Yes, I'm coming,' Margot said almost gently. 'I just don't believe it,' she murmured, still staring at Dana. 'You look so innocent, yet you've wormed your way in here and ended by deceiving us all.'

'Don't speak like that,' Jeff said sharply. 'You don't even make sense.'

'I won't let him go. I'll do something. I'll find some way to stop it!' Margot's voice was on the ascent.

'You're raving,' Jeff said curtly, and pulled her away with considerable force. At the door, he turned back to Dana. 'I'm taking my wife up to Melbourne. She'll be staying with her people ... indefinitely. There's no need to worry about a thing.' He tried to smile, but his eyes looked as if he was aware of some impending disaster.

When they had gone Dana lay back on the bed again. Within fifteen minutes she felt much better in herself, but deeply depressed. She resisted the impulse to burrow under the bedclothes and stay there. Lally would be bitterly disappointed if she failed to keep her appointment.

She jumped up, showered and dressed in tan slacks and a rye-coloured sweater, threw a suede jacket around her shoulders and went down to breakfast.

Surprisingly the day passed quickly and pleasantly in spite of some tense moments when she and Brett came into contact. He was brusque but reasonably polite, seemingly preoccupied. Dana knew she was drifting. Very soon she would have to face up to the hard facts she was only too anxious to hide from herself.

After dinner, Lally came in for a while to show

everyone the day's drawings. She handed them around, pathetically eager. Brett studied them quite seriously, making Lally his slave for ever.

'Well, these are a far cry from the usual childish daubs, young lady. I think we'd better arrange proper tuition for you.' He waited until Lally had said her goodnights, then looked directly at Dana for the first time that evening.

'Could you arrange about those lessons for the child? I'd like to pay for them. Miss Turner will have quite enough on her hands with school fees. Lally seems to have a very genuine talent, an instinctive eye for line and colour—a surprising little bundle all round.'

Dana took a deep breath. 'All right, Brett, I'd be happy to do it. Lally will be thrilled. It's one of her dreams, she was telling me.'

'Well, this is one dream we'll be able to fulfil for her.'

His thoughtfulness and generosity made Dana feel bolder. She saw the day as a day of truth. It was the time to approach Brett about Jeff, his association with Madga Ludlow. It was obvious that Jeff could or would not help himself. Magda Ludlow posed a potential threat to the Stud.

Dana did not pursue the subject then, but waited until much later in the evening when her father had gone down to check on the progress of Copper Queen, who had been brought in for foaling. Brett strolled out on to the verandah and Dan followed him.

'Brett, may I speak to you?'

'Dare I risk it?' He sounded faintly tired and irritable, an unusual state of affairs for Brett.

Dana's face clouded, but she decided to try for Jeff's sake.

'It's about Jeff!'

Brett passed a hand wearily over his eyes. 'If I live to be a hundred, you'd still be able to surprise me, Dana.'

'I'll do my best,' she said meekly, and watched with relief his face change.

'Fire away, child.' His tone was surprisingly mild. He lowered himself into a chair and watched her walk to the balcony and lean over it.

'Has Jeff never spoken to you about his troubles?' she asked quietly.

Brett gave a brief laugh. 'I know he's got them,' he said as if explaining simple logic to a child. 'You don't need a university education to work that out. But Jeff never took too kindly to being "done out of his rights", as he put it all round the town.'

'I suppose he thought he had a legitimate grievance,' Dana said cautiously, not wanting to arouse his quick temper.

'I'm afraid that's not the case, my angel. Let me explain to you briefly without going into all the facts, Jeff knew long before I did that he was out of the running for the Stud. Almost anyone else, but not Jeff. Tod spent a lifetime building up this place. He wasn't going to let it all go down the drain on Jeff. He's lost thousands on the racetrack—pounds, not dollars. His mother left him her money as well. I doubt if there's very much left of it now.' He regarded her thoughtfully for a moment. 'Tod was fond of Jeff, but he told him quite plainly that he never intended to leave the Stud to him. You can take that for a fact. I wasn't exactly thrilled to get it myself. I was happy doing what I was doing—seeing the world and getting well paid for it. Now, of course, I feel differently. The love of the thoroughbred has been installed into all of us, Jeff included.'

Dana listened in silence. She knew Brett was speaking the plain, unvarnished truth. A way of life with him. She gazed down on her hands grasping the rail. 'I don't think Jeff can help himself, Brett. He's somehow involved with ...' The name just wouldn't come out.

'Magda Ludlow,' Brett interrupted dryly. 'Hadn't you better stay out of that one?'

'But it's not like that at all,' Dana protested. 'I'm sure of it. I saw them together only once, but it left an indelible impression.'

Brett's interest was fully aroused. 'And you're positive it's not an unlikely romantic liaison. Jeff hasn't been getting much comfort at home.' His voice had a trace of bite in it.

'I'm sure,' Dana said positively.

'That leaves us with only two possibilities—love or money, and you say it's not love.' Brett shrugged in truly Gallic fashion, 'I'd think we'd better leave Jeff get out of this one on his own. He won't thank us for interfering.'

'He can't get out of it,' Dana protested fiercely. 'Some men can, some can't. Jeff can't cope.' She felt herself briefly enlightened. 'It *must* be money. She has a strong hold on him, and she's certainly not the kind of woman for whom a man madly risks his all.'

Brett laughed in genuine amusement. 'That's heartening news. You've dissipated all my cynical doubts.' His brows came together thoughtfully. 'It's just possible! It just might be possible!' he repeated forcefully, and shot a penetrating glance at Dana. 'I gather you're not of a nervous nature, my pet?' He looked at her for a moment, then swung up from his chair. 'I'm going to find Jeff.' His arm moved in a sweep. 'Maybe we can get to the bottom of this. Especially as you're so concerned for his welfare.' He sounded rather grim.

Dana sat there waiting. She wanted no more disharmony in the house, but Jeff's state of mind was undoubtedly the result of his association with a grasping woman. Poor Jeff! she thought, gazing up at the moon riding high over the fretted tops of the pines.

As if on cue Jeff came out on to the verandah. 'Brett wants to talk to me. I only hope it's not going to cause too big an upheaval!'

Dana turned her amber eyes upon him. 'I think he wants to help you, Jeff, before any real damage is done.'

Jeff's hazel eyes narrowed swiftly as he lost colour. 'You've a very strong imagination, Dana. Don't let it deceive you. I'm in no danger.'

'Please let him help you, Jeff,' she pleaded urgently. 'You *need* help, if only you'd admit it!'

Jeff sank down on a chair heavily, as if his knees were about to buckle under him. 'You don't understand, doll,' he said with deep regret. 'It's not a very pleasant story. If only you could turn the clock back!' he said with a rush of nostalgia. Harshness returned to his voice. 'You of all people wouldn't be sitting there looking at me with such compassion.'

Dana frowned. 'Why me, Jeff? What have I got to do with it?'

Jeff sat there unanswering, while the minutes slipped by. Dana had the strange sense of being alone, so deeply preoccupied was her companion. She looked up with relief as Brett came back, carrying a whisky decanter and two glasses. His voice was even, almost friendly. 'Pour yourself a drink, son. You might need it.'

Jeff did so with alacrity, tossing off the contents with the ease of long practice.

'Confession is good for the soul, they tell me,' Brett prompted. 'Start talking, Jeff. Tonight's your night! After this, I won't lift a finger to help you.'

Jeff hesitated at the dark, unyielding set of his cousin's face, then he began to speak, the words tumbling over one another, dammed up for so long they had almost choked him.

The odd thing was, Dana was not surprised. Neither, judging by his expression, was Brett. Jeff told the facts badly, making no attempt to whitewash himself, even if it were possible. It began when sheer desperation over his gambling debts had driven him into an agreement with Ray Ludlow to pull Prince Akura at his Melbourne Cup run. A skilful, highly experienced jockey, Ludlow was able to do this without any blame being attached to him.

They had amassed a small fortune over the incident, Jeff using several different contacts to place their combined bets. It was their one venture into corruption—he swore to it. He was frantic over his gambling debts—Tod had refused to help him any further—and Ray Ludlow had the misfortune to be married to a woman who had an insatiable appetite for luxury.

The only thing both men failed to take into account was her knowledge of the whole incident, or rather her brilliant guesswork, based on knowledge of her husband, which amounted to the same thing. She had used that knowledge to full effect after her husband was killed, and had been blackmailing Jeff ever since.

Jeff finished speaking abruptly and wiped his forearm over his perspiring brow. Brett put a drink at his elbow and he quickly disposed of it.

'Well, there's nothing more to be said,' Brett commented, and his voice was like iron. Jeff stood up suddenly, so that his chair went crashing to the floor. He did not even seem to notice it.

'What are you going to do?' he cried distractedly. 'I know I'm beneath contempt. God knows how I hated to pull that horse. A champion!' His eyes found Dana's and held them pleading for understanding.

Brett leaned over and set the chair straight. 'Sit down, Jeff.' It was plainly an order, and Jeff obeyed instantly. Dana looked back at him, the confused thoughts whirling around in her head until she felt too stupefied to think any more. Also her head had begun to ache abominably. Brett shot a glance at her taut profile, noting her pallor, and eased his glass towards her. 'It's your turn, now, little one. Have a shot of that. It won't hurt you.'

Dana picked up the glass automatically and sipped at it with caution. It was fiery and once down, pleasantly numbing. She continued to sip at it.

'If only I had the guts, I think I'd end it all.' There was real despair in Jeff's voice.

'Don't talk like that,' Brett said harshly. 'Get a hold of yourself, man. I'll find some way to put a stop to this.' He sounded so sure of himself that Dana and Jeff turned towards him hopefully.

'You'll pay her off?' Jeff shuddered slightly.

'Like hell I will!' Brett bit out. 'There's a pretty stiff penalty for blackmail in this country. I just might acquaint the lady with it ... personally.'

A series of expressions chased their way across Jeff's weak, handsome face, and over all a dawning hope.

'Do you mean to call her bluff? I've never been game enough to try it. You don't know her. She's vicious!'

'As long as she's not stupid too, we have a chance. And I don't think she's stupid,' Brett said heavily.

Dana put a hand to her head. 'I've got a headache,' she said plaintively, without meaning to say it at all.

For answer, Brett swung her out of her chair. 'Come along to bed, child.'

Jeff stood up, watching her go. 'I'm sorry, Dana, I really am sorry. Please believe I'm sincere.'

'I believe you, Jeff,' Dana said quietly. 'In any case, I think you've had a bad enough time of it.'

Brett kept his arm around her, then growing impatient of her hazy state of mind, swung her high in his arms. He glanced over his shoulder at Jeff. 'Stay there, Jeff. You and I have a lot of ground to cover.' It was the voice of authority. Jeff sat down again to wait for his cousin.

For the first time in a very long time, he felt a lightening of the spirit. If he did nothing else, Brett inspired confidence, emanated strength and purpose and a certain ruthlessness. Just like the old man, Jeff thought wryly, and to his surprise found himself smiling....

Up in her room, Brett laid Dana down on the bed.

'Do you think you can get out of your things?' he asked coolly.

She stared up at him in astonishment. 'You don't propose to help me?' She could feel a pulse begin to hammer away in her throat.

'Don't you think I'd be efficient?'

It was the best part of a minute before Dana could answer him.

'I don't dare think about it at all.'

He looked at her calmly. 'Try it, my dove, in the name of practicality. You look as if you might pass out at any minute.'

She swung her long golden legs off the bed. 'I assure you I won't have the slightest difficulty.'

He laughed and reached out with his right hand, tapping her cheek smartly. 'Good, then go to it. Quite frankly, my pet, you'll never make a drinker.'

'And you'll never make a gentleman!' she snapped back at him, highly incensed.

'There *is* that possibility,' Brett murmured, and walked to the door. His voice was quite solemn, but his eyes were brilliantly black.

Dana discovered she was shivering slightly. Instantly Brett became authoritative.

'Get into bed, child, though you do look very ornamental where you are, half on and half off it.'

'Brett,' she said softly, 'I've a feeling I hate you.'

'Pleasant dreams, my angel,' he said in a soothing, sympathetic voice, and shut the door on her.

Dana found it suddenly difficult to maintain her attitude of casual indifference. Brett positively unnerved her. She flopped back on the bed, turned her face down into the pillow and began to thump into it. She almost wished it was Brett!

CHAPTER THIRTEEN

BY Derby Day, the Victorian Blue Ribbon Classic, Prince Gauntlett was the talk of Melbourne, collecting the Caulfield Cup and the W. S. Cox Plate in brilliant style. Racing circles simmered with his Cup chances.

The stabilising of the big stallion was one of Sloan Gregory's greatest achievements. Days, weeks, months of constant training and attention had gone into this new off-course placidity, the dazzling on-course bursts of speed that were proving such a tremendous draw card for race patrons.

As a three-year-old, Prince Gauntlett was being schooled out of his old roguish ways and had proved consistently predictable, over a period of months, without aspiring to even-temperedness. Passion was still in evidence in his behaviour, but it was now a controlled quality.

Riding under Sloan Gregory's instructions, Mannie Boxall gave the stallion the freedom to do as he wished during a race, and he managed to do precisely the right thing. Great powerful thrusts of his hind legs carried him easily to the front and his enormous lung capacity kept him there, when the rest of the field was tiring. At the end of the race, the stallion still had plenty in reserve, demonstrating the fact with a characteristic powerful final kick.

To his trainer, the big stallion exemplified that quality of the thoroughbred which he liked to call control, the capacity to conserve his speed according to the requirements of distance. The Prince had been bred to stay and the Rankine Stud had high hopes for their top stallion's carrying off the Melbourne Cup, the greatest all-aged handicap in the world.

Dana was up very early on Derby Day, accompanying Brett and her father down to the track to watch the Prince at his early morning work-out. It was going to be fine, warm and sunny. The Prince did not care for the Wet.

Mannie put him through a bit of pacework, then galloped him for a furlong before bringing him in. A strong bond had sprung up between boy and horse that was immediately apparent. Mannie was leaning down his mount's neck, talking to him fondly and rubbing the sleek ebony coat—the same coat that he rubbed and brushed and stroked to perfection from the tall head to the neat hooves with their featherweight racing plates. They seemed to have a special affinity for each other, so pronounced that Sloan had given instructions that Mannie was to have sole charge of the stallion in his absence.

Dana watched Brett and her father, heads together, their faces very male and intent, plainly gratified by the big stallion's performance. She watched the big black horse come towards them with his beautiful swaying walk, the giant stride that was the delight of the racegoers.

'I'd say we're in line for the hat trick,' Sloan said with all his old confidence.

Brett's mouth twisted in a smile. 'Futura is running just well enough to be a danger.'

Sloan wouldn't have it, and shook his head vigorously. 'Might give him a shake. But I think Futura needs another run before he'd present any problem to our boy. I don't mind telling you, Brett, I'm confident.'

Brett glanced over at Dana and winked, and she found herself laughing. It all seemed like the culmination of a dream. She had never seen her father looking so well, so purposeful. It was obvious that he saw eye to eye with Brett. They were firm friends with a mutual regard for one another.

Mannie brought the stallion in, a grin on his tanned little face. What happened next had the quality of a nightmare. Brett put up his hand to lead the Prince in and a shot rang out from close in among the dense fringe of trees that lined the track.

The Prince reared high, then plunged, frightened by the noise. Mannie's slight body described an arc before he hit the turf, rolling and then lying still. The stallion, at any time excitable, was standing on his hind legs, his powerful forelegs thrashing the air, his white-ringed eyes rolling in his head. The sight of his raw, elemental power brought a great convulsive shudder to Dana's whole body.

Brett was only inches from the flailing hooves, but still retained the reins. Her father ran head down and crouching in the direction of the tall pines. There was a bright stillness over the track and the sun beat down in impersonal strength.

Somehow Brett was quietening the animal, keeping clear of the murderous hooves, talking, talking, all the while, gently, persuasively, confidence radiating from him. The stallion was close in to the rails now, blocked of its determination to gallop until it dropped.

Mannie still lay motionless on the other side of the rails, face down in the grass.

Dana watched Brett with a sort of half-blind dread. Her legs felt about to crumple under her. Oh, please let it bolt! she prayed fervently. What did the stallion matter when Brett looked like having his brains dashed out? Why was he so determined to hold the horse?

The morning sun seemed to penetrate her head, triggering off little trip-hammers against her temples. She could feel herself swaying and it was with a great effort that she regained her stability. Over to the right her father burst into the clearing and came to a lame halt as he watched the scene.

The rearing and plunging abruptly petered out and the stallion stood trembling under Brett's calming hand. His voice droned on interminably, almost crooning. It was impossible to make out what he was saying, but it achieved its mysterious effect.

Dana firmed her delicate jaw and breathed more deeply.

Mannie sat up, a hand to his head, very pale under his tan. 'Well!' he said slowly, then lay back on the grass again. Sloan Gregory approached them with caution, moving quietly and without haste. As he approached the horse, standing quietly beside Brett, he began to speak to him, using the same almost singing tone that Brett had used.

Eventually he was able to put the big thoroughbred on a lead while Brett moved back to Mannie. Mannie had his head turned away from them in an agony of embarrassment, being violently ill. Brett cradled the boy's head in his hands, until the worst of the bout was over.

Dana sat down on the grass. She had to. Her legs would no longer support her. She felt herself briefly dizzy.

'Are you all right, Dana?' She heard her father's

anxious voice. Tentatively she lifted her head.

'I guess so, Dad. It was just such a shock. Did they get away?'

'I'm afraid so,' her father said briefly. Mannie was shivering but declared himself fit to 'ride a winner'. Brett was not impressed. He helped the boy to his feet, keeping a firm grip on him.

'See anything at all?' He shot a glance at Sloan.

'Whoever it was, they've already departed. They must know the place pretty well, because they didn't have much time.'

'Time enough,' Brett said grimly. 'They'll already be on the highway.' He twisted his head, frowning. 'I don't know what shape Mannie is in. Concussed, I'd say.'

'All I want is me breakfast,' Mannie protested stoically. 'I'll be all right for today,' he added with a touch of defiance. He crossed over to Prince Gauntlett and put an arm around the stallion's neck. The horse pulled on the neck of his shirt almost playfully, drawing comfort from the proximity of his constant companion.

'I'll take these two back with me,' Sloan said, looking down on the little apprentice. 'I've two patients now that need attention.' He himself appeared calm and matter-of-fact, striving to put the incident behind him. 'I'd say the shot was intended to frighten the horse into bolting, perhaps doing himself an injury.'

Brett glanced back towards the trees. 'Yes, it was too bad a shot to be anything else. You'd better let a doctor have a look at Mannie. We may have to put someone else up on the Prince.'

Sloan nodded, patting Mannie's shoulder sympathetically. They started on their way back to the stables, Mannie electing to ride after the first few yards.

Dana was doing her best to appear normal, though never in her life had she known such pulverising panic. She shut her eyes against the warm golden rays of the sun, seeing only Brett's dark head, inches away from those frenzied, flying hooves.

'Dana!' Brett said abruptly.

'Yes, Brett?' she answered steadily without opening her eyes.

'You can't stay there, child. Get up!'

'Yes, of course.' She felt him take her hand and haul her to her feet, and suddenly there was the desperate need to cling to him, to feel him there—dominating, maddening, irreplaceable Brett!

He held her trembling body against him. There was something almost frightening about her tenseness.

'Dana,' he said. She didn't move. 'What is it? Tell me!'

She didn't answer. His grip on her tightened, gathering her close up against him. Her body shook with sobs. She was frightened then, too frightened to use her own voice. Her body was witness to her true emotions. No longer could she play hide and seek with the truth. Brett was as essential to her very existence as the air she breathed. She buried her head against the soft silk of his shirt, helpless and almost in a panic at her own inadequate self-control.

Brett's hand was on her hair. He was talking to her, soothing her, but she paid no heed. She burrowed against him like a child, feeding on the strength and comfort that flowed from him.

Her small clenched fist began to thump at him in pressing abandon, a protest against the risks he took, the fear they engendered in her. Brett found her fist, small in the grip of his hand, and opened it like a flower.

'Stop it, child. You'll make yourself ill.' His words steadied her, won the battle for self-control. Somewhere quite near them, the starlings had started gossiping in the fir trees. Over the horizon, the ancient hills still rolled in mighty green waves, frozen in time. The freshness of green struck the eye. So many greens, each different in every pasture, in every tree.

Dana's gaze travelled to Brett's, only to look away again. His face seemed blazingly alive, his eyes lit by many small flames. Across her own face lay a veil of sadness, an acknowledgement she had been forced into betraying herself. Her voice was strained, full of self-doubt.

'I'm sorry, Brett. You gave me a few bad moments.'

He looked down at her, his face dark and unsmiling. 'Why do you feel it necessary to apologise?'

Dana shrugged. There was a weariness in the effort. All the sorrow in the world seemed to be in the tilt of her impeccable neck, the helpless, slightly bent and delicate shoulders. She could feel his dark gaze intent upon her and knew an unbearable self-consciousness.

'I'm sorry, Brett,' she whispered huskily. 'I must go back to the house.' She turned swiftly away from him then and broke into a run. But where was there to run to? All paths seemed to lead back to Brett!

At the end of that long, eventful day, Dana picked up the evening paper again for another look at the front page. The camera had caught Prince Gauntlett's canter before the judges' stand, Mannie Boxall's happy, excited grin. Under the photograph, Jay Roberts, the veteran Turf reporter, had this to say:

'If the enemies of the big black stallion expected to ruin his chances for the Derby, they were doomed to disappointment. Prince Gauntlett leapt like a gazelle from the mobile start and in a fantastic three-furlong spurt streaked to the front like a bullet and stayed there, breaking the track record for the one and a half miles. I don't think it's too early to say: Hats off to a wonder horse!'

Dana re-read the article, then put it down, smiling. Her eyes were warm and soft, given over completely to pride in her father, in a horse, in a famous Stud. Of Brett she refused to think. She turned out the light and went to stand at the window, her head inclined and slightly tilted back to the night. The breeze was balmy against her closed eyelids, but her imagination drew a picture of an arrogant dark head, so painfully vivid that her eyes flew open in sheer self-defence.

Was this the end of her peace of mind, the old tranquillity she had taken so much for granted?

I'm over-tired, sleepy, a little crazy after such a day, she told herself fretfully. She turned away and got into bed, arranging the pillows in a comfortable position for sleep. Perhaps the best prescription for her current state of mind was to take herself off, as Jeff intended to do, body and soul to a different setting. Her life appeared to have strayed into a tempestuous sea. Only her father's presence gave it any stability.

I'll have to find some place far away from Brett, she thought tiredly, and fell asleep, full of a powerful longing.

CHAPTER FOURTEEN

THE first Tuesday in November! A day of days for all Australians since Fred Archer galloped into history on a November afternoon in 1861.

Dana opened her eyes on sunlight and soft breezes, the heady fragrance of the wattles in full golden bloom all over the Stud. Wattles and Cup fever, a twin phenomenon! She stretched her arms luxuriously above her head.

Inside her wardrobe hung her Cup outfit. She was wearing a Cecile Magnin in the professional section of Fashions on the Field, the recent controversial innovation at Flemington. She smiled to herself. Her father disliked the idea intensely. He never cared for the intrusion of commercially sponsored contests into his beloved Flemington scene, but others, like Cecile Magnin, found it a good piece of public relations for Melbourne's fashions.

The experiment had proved enormously successful, drawing huge crowds over the four-day festival. Top English and European models were invited out to assist at the Fashion judging and to represent Australia's wealth off the sheep's back by wearing an Australian Wool Board creation, and to even things up a rival representative was present wearing an ensemble of man-made fibres.

Informality had no place during Cup week when the exclusive salons of Toorak, South Yarra and Collins Street did more business in the six weeks prior to the

Cup than in all the rest of the year.

The Fashions on the Field contest carried over twenty-five thousand dollars in prize money, and every woman entering Flemington on any one of the four days of the Melbourne Cup Carnival automatically became an entrant.

Cecile Magnin, along with the rest of the fashion trade, waxed lyrical over the innovation. Not since the halcyon days when Melba had strolled across the lawn at Flemington in an exquisite creation that positively breathed London or Paris had fashion received such a fillip.

Dana's outfit was a superbly detailed suit in honeycomb linen with a vest in sharp, clear paprika. Her shoes, bag and gloves were perfectly matched to her suit and her hat was a circular upsweep of paprika stitched linen. It was the tailored look, simple and uncluttered, relying on cut and colour for its impact. On Dana it looked strikingly attractive, young and very chic, highlighting her own golden colouring.

The Stud was a hive of activity from first light. Everyone down to the last stable hand was going 'up for the Cup'. Dana scarcely saw anything of the menfolk. She had breakfast alone.

At midday, Prince Gauntlett was loaded on to the float for the trip to Flemington. Sloan Gregory and the young apprentice Mannie Boxall rode with him. They were accompanied by an armed police escort. Prince Gauntlett was in perfect form.

Dana made up and dressed with meticulous attention to detail. The eagle eyes of the judges would miss nothing, not to mention the crowds on the fence who delighted in following the girls.

When she went downstairs Jeff was already there,

immaculately tailored, fair and good-looking, checking over the contents of a bulging wallet.

For a few seconds Dana was frozen to the stairs. Jeff had given every indication of putting his life in order after Brett had rescued him from his dilemma with Magda Ludlow by the simple expedient of threatening to call in the police. Was he back at his old gambling ways? And so soon?

She moved and the stair creaked. Jeff glanced up swiftly, reading her mind in a split second.

'Not mine, doll—Brett's. He's a once-a-year punter. Just as well!' he grinned, and indicated the thick wad of notes.

Dana gave a smile of relief. She came on down the stairs and gave a quick, involuntary look in the mirror. Jeff caught her at it and smiled his admiration.

'You look wonderful, doll. You're a truly beautiful girl, Dana, inside and out.'

Brett walked in at that precise moment. From the look in his eyes he didn't appear to agree with his cousin, though he smiled a shade sardonically as he studied her slender form.

'I must confess you do look very chic,' he remarked blandly, an amused expression coming into his eyes.

'You look very *chic* yourself,' Dana said dryly, glancing at the carnation in his buttonhole. 'Both of you!' She smiled at Jeff and ignored Brett, denying herself the intense pleasure of looking at him.

Both men were superbly tailored, but Brett had an air of authority and distinction that Jeff quite missed out on. Perversely Dana slipped her arm through Jeff's. 'I hope you're going to tell me all about this wonderful new job of yours in the States.'

Jeff brightened. He glanced over her head at his

cousin, then back to Dana again. 'I have to thank Brett for it, I suppose, but just listen to this. . . .' He opened the front door with his right hand and led Dana down to the car. She listened with sincere interest to his plans to take over the running of a Kentucky stud owned by a wealthy American client of Brett's. It was, he explained, a godsend and a challenge. He needed time to find himself.

Brett gave them a few moments, then he came down to the car, slipping behind the wheel with indolent grace. His eyes turned to Dana. 'I hope it all meets with your approval?' he inquired with mock politeness, his black eyes straying over her face and shoulders.

'It's getting late, Brett,' she exclaimed, trying not to sound ruffled.

'Hah!' he said shortly, and drove very fast up to Melbourne.

Beautiful at any time, Flemington was at its floral best during Cup Week. Its famous roses rioted over the fences, masses of them, gold, pink and scarlet, with poppies, pansies and stocks, ranunculi and cinerarias in the background—a glorious show against the emerald green freshness of the lawn.

A hundred thousand people swarmed over the Course, in a high pitch of national excitement. Perhaps no less intense than when four thousand pioneers, spurred on by their love of racing, had staged a meeting over a rough bush track over a hundred years before. The Melbourne Cup, so fervently fostered by succeeding generations, was not only the richest race in the Southern Hemisphere but a deeply embedded part of the Australian way of life.

Thousands of visitors had flown into the Victorian

capital, from near and far, the rich and famous, the wealthy squatocracy, the owners of sheep stations, cattle stations, the New Zealand invasion. None dreamed of missing the Cup, a yearly ritual!

Hostesses all over the country arranged Cup parties and sweeps. In Darwin, at the Alice, from Cape York in the far North to Wilson's Promontory in the south. For the space of ten minutes, on a November afternoon, the whole nation came to a halt.

Dana strolled across the lawn with Gina Cory. Both girls were attracting many admiring glances and the occasional open comment. Gina was looking stunning in a dress and jacket ensemble of black and white figured silk with a large, floppy hat. The two girls decided the overall dressing was most impressive and managed to control their stares at the inevitable oddity and the clever publicity-seeker.

The crowds hung on the fences of the members' enclosure making broad comments on the girls, while the girls angled very determinedly to get into range of the television cameras. The weather was right and the silks and chiffons, the large, lacy picture hats, the plumes and the feathers, the flowered confections paraded across the lawn. The sun poured down over the whole scene in a shifting pattern of light and colour.

To Dana, the real excitement was in watching the horses, the gorgeous thoroughbreds that somehow managed to inspire a sense of wonder in an age full of mechanical wonders. The sun glanced off glistening spring coats, the blaze of silk, the gleam of satin. The Governor-General was escorted down the straight by massed Highland bands according to tradition and received into the Vice-regal box. The tension and excitement was mounting.

Dana found her arm being gripped almost painfully.

'Don't look now,' Gina hissed, and turned her face full on to the camera. It managed, however, to catch Dana's flawless profile. They continued walking. A petite brunette staggered past, the breeze caught under her enormous cartwheel hat loaded with cerise cabbage roses.

Over on the fence, an overseas personality was being photographed against the massed gold of the roses. A lot of interest was being displayed by the crowd. Dana became absorbed herself, watching a professional at work. That Lisa Courtney really did have something!

Gina's face, turned in the opposite direction, was glowing with pleasure. 'Why, Brett! How wonderful to see you!'

'And how wonderful you look!' he said smoothly.

Something to the left caught Dana's eye and she prepared to move off, but Brett laid a firm hand on her arm.

'I wonder if you would excuse us, Gina. Dana promised to have lunch with me. She's obviously forgotten the time.'

Gina kept her smile with difficulty. 'Of course, of course. Run along, you two,' she added playfully.

'Perhaps you'd care to join us this evening at the Victory Dinner,' Brett suggested. 'One of my guests is a highly eligible bachelor, an American, young, good-looking, *loaded*, as the saying goes. Need I say more?'

Gina smiled. 'Message received, loud and clear.' She hid her disappointment skilfully. A rich American was a rich American! And young! She watched them go, her eyes narrowed speculatively.

Brett had reserved a table for two. It was absolutely essential. The dining rooms were crowded. Melbourne people liked to entertain their guests over luncheon, either at fashionable picnic parties in the beautiful grounds, or in the glass-enclosed dining rooms.

Brett studied the wine list, conscious without even looking of Dana's mental attitude. 'No mutiny here, please,' he said dryly.

'Just testing you out.' Dana tried to sound casual.

Brett shrugged and smiled wryly. 'It won't be the smart thing to do. I'm going to keep you beside me for the rest of the afternoon.'

'But that's not possible, Brett,' she said quickly. 'I've things to attend to.'

'Then kindly postpone them. The longer you delay, the worse it's going to be for you.' Brett shot a glance at her from under frowning brows.

'I'm sure I don't understand you.' Dana raised her eyes, long and bewildered.

'Yes,' he said thoughtfully, 'that's about it. You don't.'

Dana watched while he ordered the wine, awareness nagging at her.

'Brett,' she said softly, when the waiter had gone, 'I feel we're being watched.'

'Womanly instinct?' he asked matter-of-factly.

'That, and a prickling along the nape of my neck. It's someone?' she murmured.

'It is, my pet,' he said casually. 'Margot. But if she so much as opens her mouth, I'll have her arrested.'

Dana gasped. 'Honestly, Brett, you're out of this century. The "off with their heads" era would do for a quick stab.'

'Margot, my love,' he stressed reprovingly, ignoring her comment, 'was responsible for the shot being fired at the Prince. With considerable skill, cunning and stealth,' he added dryly.

'Margot?' Dana said the name with an effort. 'But she loves horses!'

'Correction, my little innocent. Margot neither loves horses nor humans.' He turned his head slightly and focused his gaze on Margot Rankine. Its dark message sent a shiver down Margot's spine. Surely they hadn't the slightest suspicion? Her instinct told her unerringly that Brett, at least, had. Within minutes she had left the dining room.

'Drink your wine,' Brett commanded.

Dana sipped at the dry white wine, liking its sharp but delicate flavour.

'Why is it you make me feel like a fragile eighteenth-century lady being held up by a highwayman?' she asked vaguely.

Brett looked at her in some surprise, then he laughed. 'I told you before, you bring out the worst in me.'

'Never the best, do you suppose?' she asked wistfully, under the benign influence of the wine, then could have bitten her own tongue out.

His eyes narrowed appraisingly. 'Possibly under the right conditions. But not here, with a crowd of a hundred thousand around us.'

Dana set her glass down carefully, momentarily bereft of words. His words were nearly as disturbing as his look. They finished the meal in silence, each seemingly preoccupied. Out in the sunshine, Brett was hailed by a small group of acquaintances. Dana saw her opportunity to escape. She moved as quickly as possible through the swarming crowd, but not quickly enough. A lean, brown hand encircled her wrist.

'I'm not prepared to chase you all over Flemington,'

Brett drawled evenly.

Dana gave an angry exclamation. 'You're beginning to annoy me, Brett!' He glanced down at her mockingly, completely unimpressed, and Dana suffered herself to be led along, feeling hopelessly out of her depth. With Brett, she was pushed into acting the original, infantile female. He simply ignored any other style.

All along the way they were recognised, but Brett stopped for no one. No one glancing at Dana blamed him. At the entrance to the Members' car park, she managed to say: 'Where on earth are we going? Everyone and a dog is coming into Flemington and you're on your way out.'

'Come along,' Brett said, ignoring her protests. 'You wanted to see the best side of me. There's no real cause for alarm,' and Dana had no option but to follow him. They were causing quite enough attention as it was.

Ten minutes later, Brett drew up the car in a deserted, tree-lined avenue. Dana opened her eyes and gave him a long look.

'Did Dad tell you I was thinking of going overseas ... to further my career?' she rapidly improvised.

'Oh?' he murmured lazily. 'I shouldn't think you'd have to go overseas to do that.'

'Oh, but I think so,' she said steadily. 'Perhaps in the summer.'

'Do you do it on purpose?' he asked lightly, but Dana detected a faint edge to his tone.

She shook her head. 'I don't know what I'm doing,' she said with absolute truth.

'No, you don't,' he agreed with some irony. 'But I do.' With sudden decision, he reached for her, cupping her face in his hands. 'You can't run away from me, Dana. There's nowhere to run. I'm quite capable of following you around the world if I have to, but it would amount to a sheer waste of time.'

Dana closed her eyes for a moment as though concentrating, then opened them.

'But you said you didn't *like* me!'

'Isn't that the truth?' he muttered, and covered her mouth with his own. 'Kiss me, Dana,' he murmured against her soft mouth, 'or so help me I'll strangle you.'

She obeyed him at once, her lips parting on a rush of tenderness at the lover-like tones, if not the phrase.

Now, for the first time, she heard clearly the naked longing in his low, urgent voice. There was nothing gentle in that kiss, yet it held a fierce passion kept under restraint. After a while Brett lifted his head. 'You're my girl, Dana. Don't ever forget it.' His words were his own, but behind his brilliant dark eyes was the fulfilment of her cherished dreams.

'I love you, Brett,' she said clearly, her face poignant with longing.

His hand clenched hard on her shoulder, then slowly reopened. 'My God,' he said feelingly, 'what a moment you've hit on to tell me!' He leaned over and switched on the ignition. 'We'd better go back, my love, before I surely lose all control.'

Dana glanced at his taut profile, her face glowingly beautiful.

'Just you wait, Dana ... Cantrell!' Brett muttered with passionate intensity.

She looked over at him, smiling, her eyes lustrous with loving.

'I'll wait for a lifetime!' Her voice was vibrant with emotion. Their glances held for a long moment, grave, very level, and deep understanding lay between them.

In front of the Members' stand, Sloan Gregory looked around him frantically. Dana and Brett were cutting it very fine. They really couldn't delay a minute longer.

With relief, he heard Brett call his name and spun round as they came towards him.

'My God, where on earth were you....' his words died away in his throat as he gazed from one to the other. Used as he was to his daughter's beauty, he had never seen her look so heart-stoppingly lovely. A dawning wonder spread over his face.

'Well, well, well,' he said softly, his voice a little shaky. On an impulse he bent and kissed his daughter's smooth cheek, smiling over her head at his future son-in-law. 'Join me, my children,' he said swiftly, 'in watching yet another hope of mine realised ... Prince Gauntlett win the Melbourne Cup.' His eyes mirrored his complete confidence.

Down on the track, the finest thoroughbreds in Australasia lined up in the stalls for the running of the year's great event. Up in the Judges' stand, field-glasses were trained on the mobile start.

An electric silence fell over the course and a nation of twelve million people, from the densely fringed coastline to the far-flung Outback, came briefly to a halt.

Dana gripped the hands of the two most important men in the world to her, listening intently.

The starting bell sounded and the horses jumped from the stalls. There was a rush of colour, a bright blaze of silk, then came the magical words: 'They're off!'